SECRET SWEETHEART

Quinn Valley Ranch, Book 2

LIZ ISAACSON

ISBN-13: 978-1638761242

CHAPTER ONE

*B*etsy Quinn drew in a deep breath, the scent of brown sugar, maple, and the salty ham filling her nose. It was the best smell on the planet, and she couldn't help bending down to smile at the meat candy currently baking in the oven.

The kitchen at the farmhouse buzzed with activity, as the family Christmas Eve dinner was about to start. She smoothed her hair off her face and glanced at the timer on the oven. She had twenty minutes before the ham needed to be basted again.

She could easily run out to the blacksmith shop to see Knox. She tried to push the idea away, but it already had her heart beating a little faster, and while the kitchen radiated heat, the temperature inside her was what spiked.

Everyone seemed busy enough. She could sneak away. After all, Georgia already had, and her chicken noodle soup sat on the back burner of the stove, just taking up space.

"Rhodes," she said, turning to her brother as he got something out of the double-wide refrigerator. "Do you need me to go get Granny and Gramps?"

"No, I'll go grab them. I need to get my presents from my cabin anyway." He barely looked at her. The only time Betsy found the spotlight among her family was during mealtimes. It shouldn't matter so much to her, but providing good food and getting complimented on it really meant something to her.

Betsy backed up a step, almost expecting Cami to say something to her. Ask her where she was going. Something. Her younger sister didn't even look her way.

So Betsy spun on her heel and hurried into the mudroom off the side of the kitchen. She shoved her feet into a pair of snow boots that were two sizes too big and put on her coat. She hustled outside as she zipped it up, because she only had a few minutes.

The glowing, yellow lights in the buildings on the ranch brought a sense of comfort to her she hadn't known she needed. She'd felt unsettled these past few months, and in the quiet moments before she went to bed, she allowed herself to admit the exact date everything in her life had been put in a blender and then turned on high.

The day Knox Locke had been hired at Quinn Valley Ranch.

She'd immediately gotten his number, as she had all the ranch hands' numbers. She texted them in a group so they'd know if she'd have lunch at the homestead that day or not. She'd been immediately entranced by his dark green eyes, a more subdued version of his twin's.

Betsy's steps slowed. She couldn't date her sister's boyfriend's brother. Could she?

Probably should talk to Georgia about it, she thought. But she didn't turn back, and Georgia was going through a tough time with Logan right now anyway. They weren't exactly together anymore, and Betsy's heart took courage.

If Georgia wasn't dating Logan, she had no reason to object to Betsy starting something with Knox.

But every step Betsy took along the cleared path toward the blacksmith shop testified of something different. Pushing aside the doubts, she stuck her hands in her pockets, hoping for a bit of warmth. December in Idaho possessed a kind of icy brutality that pockets could not stave off.

The blacksmith shop will be warm. The thought drove her to move faster, and as she approached, she slowed. She felt like someone had tied her to a yo-yo in October, when Knox had shown up on the ranch wearing that delicious gray cowboy hat and saying he was their new farrier.

She'd texted him and asked him what he was doing for Christmas, and he'd said he had a ton of work to do for the new year since he was leaving town for a couple of weeks immediately following the holiday.

After that, he'd messaged. *I'm going home for dinner.*

He hadn't asked her to come visit him. He never did, but Betsy felt fireworks between them every time they were in the same room together. And it was time to find out if Knox did too.

"If he doesn't, fine," she whispered to herself, her breath steaming into a thick cloud in front of her. "You'll find someone else." That statement was ridiculous, as Betsy rarely left the ranch and hadn't dated in...she couldn't even remember how long. She went to church with her family, and she'd met a man here and there over the years.

But nothing had ever sparked as hotly as the flame between her and Knox. As evidenced by what had happened in the kitchen, her excitement for him grew just by thinking about him.

Still, she stood at the door of the blacksmith shop without going in. Would he think her too forward?

Now or never, she thought, the cold pressing down on her now. The tips of her ears would be frostbitten if she didn't either go into the shop or hurry back to the house. She checked her phone—only twelve minutes left before the timer on her ham went off, and someone would know she'd snuck out.

She raised her hand to knock, deciding to be brave and really pound on the door. Her fist swung down at the same time the door opened, and she ended up punching Knox in the face.

He grunted and groaned and fell back a couple of steps. Both of his hands went to his face, and horror struck Betsy behind the ribs.

"Oh, no," she said. "I'm so sorry." Blessed warmth emanated from the shop, and she rushed forward to help him. "I'm sorry, Knox. I was just knocking to see if you were here."

"I'm here," he said through his fingers. He touched his nose, and his fingers came away blood-free. He inhaled and sniffed and met her eye.

Those fireworks went off, and Betsy stilled. The man before her had never indicated that he liked her for more than the woman who fed him sometimes. Perhaps there had been a moment or two over the past two and a half months where his gaze had lingered on her. Maybe an extra smile. Some late-night texting.

Or maybe she'd hallucinated those instances because she'd been crushing on him since his arrival on the ranch.

"Ready for your trip?" she asked, mentally kicking herself for such a stupid conversation topic. She was thirty-four-years-old, and she should be better at flirting with a man. Letting him know that she was interested, so that the ball was in his court.

"Yep," he said with a slow smile. "How's the party prep coming?"

She glanced at her phone again. "I have about nine minutes before I have to be back." She took a step closer to him. "I just thought...." She couldn't finish, because she had no idea what to say. Or what she'd been thinking.

Foolishness raced through her, and Knox obviously had more experience with relationships than she did, because he said, "I was just heading out. Want to walk back up with me?"

"Yes," she said, relief raging through her. She flashed him a tight smile and kept her hands clenched into fists in her pockets.

"What did you make for dinner?" he asked, following her out of the shop and turning back to lock it.

"Maple and brown sugar glazed ham," she said. "We all make our own dishes, and they somehow come together into a meal."

"Sounds nice," he said.

"You could stay," she said, immediately wanting to glue her lips together. She already knew he was going to his parents' house. They'd already talked about this.

Knox looked at her, a curious edge in his eyes that could barely be seen through the thickening darkness. "I'm going to miss you while I'm gone." He smiled at her, and the walk back to the house happened with clouds beneath her feet.

"Have fun on your cruise," she said as she paused with her foot on the bottom step.

He chuckled, the sound rumbling through her chest in the best possible way. "Yeah, me, my brother, and my parents. Going to be a real riot."

"Is Logan going?"

"He was," Knox said. "But then a job came up. So no, not this time."

Betsy nodded, her smile seemingly stuck in place. "See you when you get back."

"I hope so," Knox said, and Betsy seized onto that hope and took it with her back into the homestead.

She'd just hung her coat on the peg when the timer went off. She darted around the corner and pulled her ham out of the oven. She basted the meat and ran a knife along all the slices.

"Dinnertime!" she called, and people got up from the couches and came into the kitchen. While she'd been gone, Rhodes had gone down the road to the cabins near the entrance, and Granny and Gramps shuffled forward to survey the food spread on the counter.

Wheat bread, chicken noodle soup, scalloped potatoes, and ham. And of course, Rhodes's corn and bacon dip. Betsy had given up the argument that an appetizer wasn't really part of the meal, because Rhodes didn't care what she thought—at least about this.

"Hey, Granny," she said, linking her arm through her grandmother's.

"There you are, dear," she said. "I didn't see you when I got here."

Betsy's whole body flushed. *I'm going to miss you while I'm gone.* "I ran outside to say good-bye to a friend," she said just as a man moved in front of her.

"Logan," Betsy said with a healthy dose of surprise in her voice. "What are you doing here?"

"Oh," Georgia said, stepping out from behind the kitchen counter. "Everyone, Logan and I made up. He's here for dinner." She beamed at him, and Betsy welcomed him back even as her heart sank all the way to her toes. Maybe all the way into the floor.

They'd made up. She should be happy for her sister—and she was.

But it put her and Knox on fragile ground again. Thankfully, her mother engaged Logan in a conversation, sweeping him away from Betsy so she could allow the smile to slip from her face.

Everyone started serving themselves, and Betsy stood back the way she always did during mealtime. "Want me to get you something, Granny?"

"Soup and ham," she said. "And that bread, and as much dip as will fit on the rest of the plate."

Betsy giggled and picked up a plate and a bowl for her grandmother. "It's no secret what you like," she said, shaking her head.

"Well, some secrets are worth keeping," Granny said. "And some aren't." She picked up a napkin and the silverware she needed.

Betsy looked at Granny and then focused on ladling some soup into her bowl. "What are you saying?"

"Was that Knox I saw leaving just before you came in?"

"I didn't come in," Betsy said, the lie bitter on her tongue. She glanced down the line, but Gramps was behind Granny, and he was still buttering a slice of Jessie's honey whole wheat bread.

Her eyes met Granny's again, and the older woman just smiled. "Oh, okay. I see how it is." She touched her lips in the universal sign of a secret. "It'll be our little secret."

"I appreciate that," Betsy said, almost under her breath. "It's just…."

"I know what it is," Granny said after a few seconds of silence. "Like I said, some secrets are worth keeping, and some aren't. Maybe this one is, at least for a little while."

Betsy finished loading the plate with the food her grandmother wanted and took it to the table for her. She returned to the line and got herself some food before sitting down. Logan, of all people, sat right beside her and picked up his fork.

"So are you and Knox dating?" he asked, point blank.

"What?" Betsy scoffed though a path of worry burned through her with the speed of a racecar. "No." She laid her napkin on her lap. "He's the farrier and I see all the cowboys when they come to the homestead for meals."

She turned away from him, her heart hammering in her chest. Had he seen her and Knox outside too? Had Knox said something to him? Jessie sat on her other side, and she said, "Hey, Jess. How's that new software working?" Her sister managed the herd, the pregnancies, and the sale of cattle, and she'd just gotten a new tracking system a few weeks ago.

Jessie answered, but Betsy honestly didn't hear her. Granny's words drifted through her mind. *Some secrets are worth keeping.*

So she'd keep her crush on the gorgeous Knox Locke a secret. No problem. She could do that.

Couldn't she?

CHAPTER TWO

*K*nox found it entirely unfair to go from Caribbean warmth to Idaho chill in the same day. His body was having a hard time acclimating and keeping up with the changes, and he held his hands in front of the fire in the blacksmith shop at Quinn Valley Ranch.

He'd been gone since Christmas Eve, and he'd missed the New Year's celebration too. Honestly, he was fine with all of that. The Quinn's were great people, but he sometimes got overwhelmed with the sheer number of them.

His mind focused on a particular Quinn he'd like to spend some alone-time with, but now that Logan was back with Georgia, Knox felt Betsy slipping further and further from his reach. Not that he'd ever reached out to her.

He sighed and turned away from the fire. He didn't have a whole lot to do for Quinn Valley this afternoon, because he'd spent his last working hours before the cruise getting everything done. He'd spent the day at Granite Springs Ranch, but they didn't even have a smithy, and he needed the one here to complete his jobs at the other ranch.

Behind him, the door opened, and he turned that way to

see Newton Matthews enter. "Hey, Knox," he said, adjusting his hat and pausing just inside the door. "I thought I saw smoke out here."

"I'm sure you did." Knox smiled at the other cowboy and crossed the small space to shake his hand. "And it's about ten below freezing out there."

"So cold," Newt said, entering further and closing the door behind him. "I know you just got back, but I'm wondering if you want to step into my place for the poker game tonight."

Knox's eyebrows went up. He'd been working at Quinn Valley for about three months now, and because he wasn't terribly outgoing and loud—and worked in the blacksmith shop alone most of the time—he was still getting to know everyone at the ranch.

He knew Newton from high school, and when Betsy made lunch for everyone, he usually sought out the dark-haired cowboy so he'd have someone he knew to sit by.

"Poker?" he asked.

"Yeah, it's casual," he said with a shrug. "But we're supposed to get a replacement if we can't come, and I just got a date with Parvati." He grinned like he'd figured out how to achieve world peace instead of getting a date with a woman. Of course, Knox hadn't exactly been able to ask anyone out in a while either.

He only had one person he wanted to get to know better anyway, and his nose twitched a little with the memory of Betsy punching him in her attempt to knock on Christmas Eve. A smile curved his lips, and he wasn't sure if it was for her or because Newt had gotten a date with the woman he liked.

"I can do it," he said.

"Great," Newt said. "Everyone brings something to eat. It's casual, like I said. No real money changes hands."

"Good," Knox said. "Because I can't remember the last time I played poker."

"Probably at scout camp when we were fifteen." Newt laughed, and Knox joined him.

"Probably."

"Starts at seven. It's out in the east stables." He turned to go. "I'll tell Clay you're stepping in for me."

"Sounds good." Knox held the door for Newt as he left, and when he turned back to the blacksmith shop, all he could think about was what snack he should bring to poker night with the other cowboys that night.

Clay Martin ran the veterinary care at the ranch, and while Knox didn't know him well, he'd seen the man eat eight chocolate chip cookies at the Harvest Festival last fall. There was only one bakery in town, and surely Knox could get a bunch of cookies.

He immediately started to worry if cookies were too simple, and he ended up completing his work for the other ranch and zipping into town, dozens of ideas for food coursing through his mind.

Skipping the bakery, he went to the grocery store instead. When his own mouth watered at the sight of the seven-layer dip, he knew he'd found his snack. Two containers of that and three bags of chips later, and he was on his way back to the ranch.

The east stables sat pretty far east on the ranch, and he wondered why the men set the game up out there. Maybe Rhodes didn't know about it. Newt had said that money didn't exchange hands, but that didn't mean the foreman would approve of poker on his property.

Nerves danced through Knox as he pulled up to the stables. Bright, cheery light leaked out from underneath the door, and he could hear people laughing inside. For some reason, his steps slowed.

He'd always felt like the tarnished version of his brother Logan. Where he had bright green eyes, Knox's were muted. Logan could grow a healthy beard in a week while Knox struggled to even have his look good after a couple of months. Logan had charisma; Knox knew how to hide in the shadows.

The scent of barbecue met his nose, and he suddenly wondered if he'd brought the right food. Why hadn't Newt told him what to bring?

He reached the door and couldn't prolong entering unless he was willing to go on home by himself. He didn't want to do that either, as Logan let his dogs outside and then back in, so they tracked snow and mud all over the kitchen.

Nudging the door with his foot, it swung open easily to reveal a round card table had been set up in the middle of the open area before the stalls took over. A separate table held the food, and a few other people stood there, eating and laughing while a radio warbled country music from a higher shelf.

"Oh, hey," Clay said, separating from the group and coming over to Knox. "Newton said you'd be taking his place." He looked down at the seven-layer dip in Knox's hands. "Oh, stars alive. Flynn is going to love you." He grinned and took a couple bags of chips from Knox. "Guys, Knox is here. He's playing for Newton tonight."

Knox said hello to Flynn Hollister, who took the seven-layer dip and said it was all for him. At least Knox knew he'd earned one friend.

Another cowboy—still dressed in his jeans, boots, hat, and belt buckle—Wyatt Barlow grinned and stepped out of the way so Knox could see the last man.

Except it wasn't a man at all.

Betsy stood there, stirring something in a Crock pot that wasn't plugged in anymore. She tucked her gorgeous red-tinted blonde hair behind her ear before she looked up at him. "Hey, Knox."

He could've fallen over with the level of flirtatiousness in her voice. Instead, he simply stared. If anyone else noticed the exchange, they didn't say anything.

Clay clapped him on the back and said, "We start in five minutes. So everyone get your food, and let's get this game going."

"I hope you boys are ready to lose tonight," Betsy said without taking her eyes off of Knox. "I'm feeling real lucky."

The other cowboys laughed, and Knox startled when he realized he'd fallen into a trance. He joined his half-hearted laughter to theirs, loaded up his plate, and took the last seat at the table.

It happened to be directly across from Betsy, and he wondered if he was torturing himself on purpose. She felt so out of his league. Completely off-limits, as she was his boss's sister and his brother's girlfriend's sister.

But, oh, how his heart ricocheted around in his chest at the very sight of her. Tonight, she wore a blouse the color of blueberries, and it went so well with her hair. He rarely saw her wear it down, and as she scraped it together into a pony-tail, he mourned the loss of it.

She cracked her knuckles and picked up her barbecue pork sandwich. "All right. Let's play." She shuffled the cards like a pro, and that made Knox's pulse accelerate even more.

He managed to eat while keeping one eye on her while she dealt, all the while wondering how he could be the one to take her back to the homestead when the game ended.

CHAPTER THREE

Betsy contained the excitement at seeing Knox by shuffling extra hard and then practically throwing the cards around the table as she dealt. Knox Locke, sitting right in front of her. It was like God had heard her thoughts and listened to her prayers, and then answered them.

Thank you, Lord, she thought as she finished dealing and picked up her own hand. She was exceptionally skilled at poker, and everyone but Knox knew it. She felt them all watching her, but she pretended like she didn't.

She moved one card over, and then another one to the front before looking up. "Bets in." She reached for the bowl of peanut M&Ms in the middle of the table and took a handful for her own betting bowl. Everyone else did too, Knox the slowest and last to figure out that they used the candy to play.

Clay picked up the bowl of chocolate and set it by him, and if Betsy didn't watch him like a hawk, he'd eat it all before the night was through. Everyone put one piece in to play, and then the real fun started.

She'd been playing poker with these guys for a few years

now, and she had all their tells memorized. She could see Wyatt's bluff from a mile away, and called him on it in the second round.

Her cards won, and she swooped all the candy toward her with a cackle. Clay dealt next, and Betsy didn't get great cards. She traded out a couple of them and decided to play with what she had, though it wasn't win-able. She could tell by Clay's sniff that his weren't great either, and Flynn's ducked head meant that he was trying to decide if he should even play the hand.

Knox she hadn't figured out yet. He still looked a bit like he'd been hit in the face with a frying pan, his eyes a bit wider than normal and constantly scanning the table, watching what everyone else was doing.

She actually admired that, because he wasn't loud or obnoxious. Of course, she'd never seen him speak louder than necessary, and he emanated a cool, quiet strength she really liked given her family's loud, tense nature.

Sure enough, Flynn folded and Wyatt kept driving the bid up until Clay dropped out. Knox did just after that too, and Betsy studied Wyatt to see if he really had something or not. He stared back at her with his dark eyes, giving nothing away.

Which totally gave away that his cards could beat hers. "Fold," she said, and he whooped. He placed his cards face-down on the table, and Clay immediately grabbed for them.

"A pair of eights," he said with disgust, throwing the cards toward Wyatt, who was still scooping his winnings toward him.

Betsy shook her head. She couldn't have beaten a pair of eights, but Wyatt had tricked her into thinking he had something really good. So she'd watch him closer. Bluff back.

Her eyes moved to Knox, and she couldn't bluff her way out of the blush that heated her face when she found him watching her too. Their gazes locked, and she probably wouldn't have known if the Yellowstone geysers blew up and started melting the planet. It would still just be her and him in this moment, because she saw something in his eyes she'd never seen before.

Maybe she hadn't been looking. Maybe he'd been really good at hiding how he felt. Maybe, maybe, maybe.

But no matter what maybe she landed on, Betsy could definitely see that Knox held an edge of heat and desire in his eyes. The same desire she felt flowing through her blood like liquid lava.

A card landed in front of her, breaking their connection. She cleared her throat under the louder noise of Flynn saying he better get something good this time and picked up her cards. She'd always loved her time in the east stables, playing poker. It got her out of the homestead, for one. And for another, she always felt like she was worth more than the last dish she'd prepared.

Sure, the cowboys loved what she brought to poker night, but she'd also been known to drive into town and buy several bags of candy and call it good. They were okay with that too.

As the game continued and she won again and then again, Betsy couldn't help thinking about the homestead. What would happen when her father retired for good and Rhodes wanted to move into the house where she and all her sisters lived? What if he met someone and fell in love, and they wanted the homestead to start raising their own family in?

Betsy had always known she wouldn't be able to live in the homestead forever, but a certain level of fear had started to constrict inside her whenever she thought about leaving it. Mostly because she had no idea where she'd go or what she'd do.

"I'm beat," Clay finally said, throwing down his last hand. "And my stomach hurts."

Betsy looked at the empty bowl of ante and started laughing. "You're such a pig, Clay," she said through her chuckles, and everyone got up and started cleaning up the table.

"Does Rhodes know you guys play poker out here?" Knox asked as he sidled up next to her at the table.

"Oh, sure," she said. "He doesn't care, as long as I bring him some of the spoils." She grinned up at him, momentarily blinded by his good looks and close proximity. It may have been her imagination, but her voice sounded full of only breath when she said, "That's why I took him his own container of pulled pork earlier this evening."

"Smart." Knox smiled at her, and that moment came flaring back to life. "Do you need help getting all of this back to the homestead?"

"Yeah," she said, seizing onto the opportunity to spend some time alone with him. "That would be great."

He moved away, leaving a cold space at her side, to help with the table and chairs, and before she knew it, everything was cleaned up and everyone was ready to go.

The other cowboys loaded up in their trucks and left while Knox was still helping her put the leftover buns and the Crock pot half-full of meat in her backseat. Depending on what she brought, she sometimes walked from the homestead. But not with pulled pork, and certainly not in the winter.

"I'll follow you over," he said, stepping over to his truck. Betsy got behind the wheel of her car and inched down the road, her nerves firing like someone had poured red ants into her brain.

"Calm down," she told herself. "He's not going to kiss you or anything." She wasn't sure if she swooned or blacked out for a moment at the very thought, but the next thing she knew, her car drifted and then full-on slid into the snowbank. A horrible, metallic crunching sound met her ears, and she got thrown over the steering wheel.

Once she'd come to a stop, she blinked out the windshield into the darkness, trying to figure out what had happened.

And then the man she'd been dreaming about kissing opened the door and peered inside. "Are you okay? There's a really icy patch right there."

Yeah, sure. An icy patch. Betsy nodded and got out of the car, sticking her hands in her coat pockets so they didn't freeze. "Will you just take me home?" she asked. "I can have the boys deal with this in the morning."

"Sure thing." Knox walked with her to the passenger side of his truck and helped her up and into it. Then he returned to her car and collected the food before joining her. "How often do you guys play poker?"

"Once a month," she said, taking a deep breath of this space that was so full of the smell of him. Cologne and pine and burnt metal. She'd never get enough of it. "Did you have fun?"

"Yeah," he said. "Surprisingly, I had a great time."

"Surprisingly?"

"Yeah, well, monthly poker night isn't really my thing." He barely moved the truck down the icy roads, and they were probably going five miles an hour.

"I thought you did great."

He chuckled, the sound sending tremors through her body. "Are you kidding? By my count, you won all but two hands."

"You counted?"

He cut a quick glance at her, and dang if that didn't light her up like Times Square. Not that she'd ever been to Times Square. But she knew it had a lot of lights. "I'm just observant," he said.

"Sure, okay," she teased, liking this tether between them. Her phone lit up, distracting her, and she groaned when she saw Rhonda Drexel's name on the screen.

"What?" Knox asked.

Betsy turned her phone over and looked out the window. "Just something for the Valentine's dance." A completely fantastical thought entered her mind. "Hey, you should sign up for the bachelor auction for the festival."

He belly laughed then, and the sound was so bright and cheerful that Betsy couldn't help smiling. "I just said I didn't really do poker nights. And you want me to get up in front of women and be bid on?" He shook his head and chuckled some more. "You're out of your mind."

"You don't think people would bid on you?"

He turned down the road that led to the homestead, and Betsy sensed her time with him was almost up. "No, Betsy. I don't think the women of this town would bid on me."

I would. The words filled her mind. Screamed in her ears. She swallowed, trying to hold them in. Knox parked in front of the homestead and unbuckled his seatbelt.

"I would," Betsy blurted before he could get out of the truck. "I'd bid on you, Knox."

His attention swung toward her, almost in slow motion, while she tried to figure out what she'd just said. His eyebrows went up. "Yeah?"

She nodded, suddenly desperate to get out of the truck. She grabbed the package of hamburger buns between them and opened her door. He met her at the front of the truck with the Crock pot and walked up the steps with her to the front door.

Inside, she said, "Just set that on the counter," which he did while she tossed down the buns and started to unwind her scarf. She hung her winter clothes on a hook in the mudroom, noting the silence and stillness in the homestead that night.

Either poker had gone later than she'd thought or her sisters were downstairs watching a movie. Betsy was glad it was quiet, that she didn't have anyone to tell about the night's events quite yet.

Knox waited for her in the kitchen, and anticipation squirreled through her. "Do you want to stay for coffee?" she asked.

"It's almost ten-thirty at night," he said quietly, those foresty eyes delving right into her soul, learning all her secrets.

"Oh, right. I—" She went mute when he stepped into her personal space and took her hand in his. She looked down to see their fingers joined, and she enjoyed the river of heat as it cascaded over her entire body.

"It's good to see you, Betsy," he said, his voice nothing more than a husky whisper. He leaned down and pressed his lips to her forehead. Cold as his mouth was, it still sent sparks flying down her spine.

He pulled his hand away and fell back a step. Their eyes met, and that magnetic attraction between them flared to life. "I'll see you later." He turned and walked toward the front door as if he'd held her hand and kissed her countless times before. Not too rushed, not too slow.

"Knox?" she called when he put his hand on the doorknob.

He twisted back toward her. "Yeah?"

"When will I see you again?"

A smile touched his mouth and crinkled those beautiful eyes. "Maybe next week. I'm out at Granite Springs this weekend."

She nodded. He ducked his head and walked out, leaving her with the glow and warmth of his touch.

There was no way she was going to be able to sleep tonight, which meant she'd probably get roped into doing something she didn't want to do at tomorrow's Valentine's Festival planning meeting.

CHAPTER FOUR

*K*nox was bent behind a horse the first time his phone went off. He ignored it and exhaled, his breath fogging in the air in front of him. Betty Boop, this horse he currently had resting almost all of her weight on his thigh, couldn't be given an inch or she'd kick him.

So he didn't flinch when his blasted phone rang again. He kept filing, finally getting Boop's hoof into the shape it needed to be in. He'd measured her yesterday and bent the horseshoes at the smithy at Quinn Valley Ranch in the afternoon.

They hammered on like a dream, and he released her with a pat on the rump. "Go on, girl," he said as she huffed and walked away. "Yeah, I feel like that too," he muttered after her, looking at his tools that littered the ground.

He inhaled deeply and ignored the twitch of pain in his back as he bent to clean up. Betty Boop was the last horse of the day out here at Granite Falls, and he really needed something to eat before he started gnawing on his own arm.

His phone vibrated as he moved, reminding him that he'd missed some calls. He pulled out his device and checked it, finding Logan to be the culprit. He'd even left a message, but Knox ignored that and navigated to the texts first.

Where are you? I need you at the community center.

Knox frowned at the words, imagining them to be said with terseness and frustration. Instead of barking something back via text to his twin, Knox called Logan.

"Hey," he said easily when Logan picked up. "I'm down at Granite Falls, working."

"Well, I've got a job for you at the community center."

Knox blew out his breath, more perturbed with Logan than usual. He felt like his brother had beaten him to the punch—again. Gotten the girl first, even if it wasn't the same girl.

"I don't need a job," Knox said. "I'm busier than I even have time for." He'd been contracted to work at three farms and ranches in the Quinn Valley area, and it was a juggling act to keep his trio of bosses satisfied.

"Trust me, you want this one," Logan said. "So you'll be here in twenty minutes."

"No," Knox said. "I'm stopping for lunch."

"I'll buy you lunch."

Knox opened his mouth to argue but paused. Logan was offering to buy him lunch? This must be serious. Still, he sighed in a long hiss. "Fine," he said. "But I want it waiting for me when I get there. I'm *starving*."

"You'll have your lunch. Get here quick." Logan ended the call before Knox could yell to him to go down the street to Bacon Boys, the best burger joint in a hundred miles, maybe more.

If twins really did have some sort of freaky powers of communication, he hoped Logan would hear him as he said, "Double bacon stacker," as he picked up the last of his tools and tucked them in his apron. "Candied bacon fries. The biggest Diet Mountain Dew they have."

His throat itched in the worst way, and he couldn't feel his fingertips as he started for his truck. By the time he pulled up to the community center, he'd realized that he hadn't checked in with Liam before he'd left the ranch. His boss on the small operation said he had something for Knox and to stop by the homestead before he left.

Tomorrow, he told himself as he got out of the truck. The sky was intensely blue without a cloud in sight. Because of that, the cold that attacked his lungs felt like knives stabbing through his chest.

He hurried toward the entrance of the community center, his stomach roaring at him for meat and cheese and bacon. Logan pushed out of the doors before Knox could get there, and he held up a bag from Bacon Boys.

Relief flooded Knox, and he swiped the food from his brother with a grin. His twin was also smiling like a fool, and Knox cocked his head. "What's with you?"

"Come see."

"See what?" Knox didn't come to the community center very often, because he wasn't interested in yoga classes or pickleball or making pies.

Logan didn't answer; he simply went back inside. Knox followed, opening the bag and grabbing a couple French fries. They didn't come out well because of all the cheese, but he managed to get a bite of food into his mouth.

He groaned at the salty, crispy potatoes, which earned him a chuckle from his brother. Logan went into the small gymnasium behind the check-in desk, and when Knox entered too, he saw several tables set up along the perimeter, with people milling about.

"What is this?" he asked, digging past the fries for the burger. He could eat that one-handed if he had to.

"There was a meeting today for the Valentine's Festival," he said. "And they need volunteers."

Knox frowned. "So what? I don't have time to volunteer."

"Well, I already signed us up for the construction of a dance floor and to fix the stage. It's got a lot of rot they just found."

"Logan," Knox said, peeling the paper back on his double bacon stacker. "You're the carpenter."

"But I *need* your help," he said.

"You do not. You could build a house from the ground up all by yourself."

Logan nudged Knox, almost knocking the burger out of his hands. He threw him a dirty look, only to find him grinning at someone across the gym. Knox followed his gaze, the burger really slipping from his fingers when he saw Betsy Quinn standing there with her sister.

"Whoa there, bro," Logan said, steadying Knox's burger. "Now do you get it? I think she signed up to work on the dance. Hint, hint."

Knox tore his gaze from Logan. "But you're dating Georgia."

"So what?" Logan asked. "Believe it or not, Betsy and Georgia aren't the same person."

"You don't think it's weird?" He bit into his burger, forgetting everything but the taste of that fatty meat and that melted, American cheese. Oh, yeah. This trip to town had been well worth it, especially because he'd gotten this burger for free.

"No," Logan said. "I don't think it's weird, and I know you like her."

Knox wanted to ask him how he knew, but the needs of his stomach won out over asking questions. When he finished the burger and wiped his fingers clean, he said, "Betsy said she'd bid on me if I did the bachelor auction."

Logan's eyebrows shot toward his cowboy hat. "Are you going to do the auction?'

"Heavens, no," Knox said with a scoff. "I don't need to embarrass myself in front of anyone." Least of all the gorgeous Betsy Quinn. He looked at her again, seeing that she'd moved to a different table. "You really don't think it's weird if I ask her out?"

"Do you like her?"

Knox shrugged. "I mean, I guess." It sounded like a lie even to him.

"Go sign up for the dance," Logan said, nudging him again.

Knox was tired of being elbowed, so he took his French fries and crossed the gym to the table beside Betsy. The sign-up sheets there were for the bake-off and the Valentine decorating. Both of those were a hard pass for Knox, and he casually moved over to the next table.

He breathed in and out before Betsy said, "Knox," with a heavy dose of surprise in her voice.

"Oh, hey," he said reaching for the pen next to the sign-up sheet to help with the dance. Her name sat several lines up, and dang, if his heartbeat didn't pitter around in his chest. He managed to scrawl his name on the next blank line while he said, "How did your meeting go?"

"Oh, it was fine," she said, and he knew she was being kind.

"Most meetings aren't great," he said.

"I like Pastor Dahl's meetings."

"Yeah?" he asked, not really a church-goer himself. At least as of last Sunday. If Betsy went, maybe Knox would consider dragging his weary bones out of bed and putting on a tie in a couple of days.

Betsy faced him now, her eyes tracking a woman who came to the table and collected the sign-up sheets. He'd gotten here just in time. "He says good things," she said. "It's never more than an hour, and it gets me off the ranch."

Knox met her eyes, searching her face for more meaning than what she'd said. "You don't get off the ranch much?"

"Not really," she said, bumping him with her hip. He was starting to wonder if he had a sign that said *Nudge me* taped somewhere on his body. "I mean, you cowboys are a hungry bunch, you know?"

Knox smiled at her. "I love it when you make lunch for us."

"Oh, I do too," she said. "But my life seems to rotate around the ranch."

He wasn't sure, but he thought he caught a hint of emotion in her voice. Whether she was happy or sad about her life being wrapped up in Quinn Valley Ranch, he wasn't sure.

"Betsy, we need to go." Georgia looked at Knox. "Hey, Knox. Good to see you."

"You too, Miss Georgia." He tipped his hat at her as Betsy laced her arm through her sister's.

"Well, maybe we'll work together on the dance," he said.

Betsy's aqua eyes glittered at him like sunlight bouncing off water. "I hope so."

She might as well have shot him with Cupid's arrow—straight through the heart. He watched her walk away, sending up a quick prayer that he could figure out how to hook and keep a woman like Betsy Quinn.

CHAPTER FIVE

*B*etsy mixed the flour together with the eggs to make the pasta dough, gently kneading it all together the way Granny had taught her. She didn't need to make homemade noodles for her famous four-cheese chicken and veggie ravioli, but it sure was better when she did.

All she could think about while she worked was Knox's statement that he liked it when she cooked for the cowboys. She'd deliberately skipped Monday and Tuesday, and not just because the smithy sat cold and dormant on those days. Fine, maybe she'd checked to see if Knox would be at the ranch before deciding that today was the day to feed everyone. The day *had* dawned with the thought of ravioli in her head, so that was what everyone at Quinn Valley Ranch would get.

"These vegetables are done," Granny said from her spot in front of the stove. In her old age, she leaned one palm against the counter while she stirred, and Betsy felt a flash of love for her grandmother hit her.

"All right," she said. "I'll get the cheese. Then we can add the chicken." She'd pulled out one of the leftover bags she'd frozen from an earlier meal. Because she'd saved all that time, she was totally justified in taking the time to make the pasta from scratch.

The pan hissed and fizzled when she added the ricotta, and Granny stirred everything around. "How are you and Knox?"

"Granny," Betsy chastised, glancing around. No one else was even in the house. Jessie and Cami were out in the ranch administration meeting with Rhodes and the other ranch hands. Georgia had probably gone to visit the pigs, though the January temperatures stung the nose and toes. "There is no me and Knox."

"Oh, so we're still in secret mode."

"There's nothing to tell. No secret." Betsy hadn't told anyone about the smoldering look she and Knox had shared during the poker game, or the situation in the kitchen with the hand-holding and the kiss. He hadn't texted her at all since then, though he had shown up at the community center and signed up to help with the Valentine's dance.

Secretly, Betsy imagined herself with Knox all the time. Walking down the cleared lanes, their scarves and coats buttoned and tied up tight, their fingers intertwined.

The back door opened, breaking into her fantasies. Betsy said, "Not a word to Mom."

Granny made a locking motion against her lips and glanced up as Betsy's mother came into the kitchen. "Whew," she said. "It is so cold out there. I hope I didn't kill the yeast on the walk over." She slid two sheet pans onto the kitchen counter and exhaled heavily. "Smells good in here."

She and Betsy traded places as she stepped over to the stove to check on the filling, and Betsy moved to separate the sheet pans so they could start to warm evenly. Her mouth watered at the thought of warm rolls and butter, and she stepped over to the fridge to find the apricot rhubarb jam she'd made last fall.

"How are things going with the Valentine Festival?" her mother asked, shrugging out of her coat.

"We haven't met yet," Betsy said. "Well, we did. Once. But there were only three of us, and they hadn't put out their volunteer sign-ups yet." She expected a text from Rhonda any day now, and she hoped she and Knox would be able to work together.

You already work together, she told herself, giving herself a mental shake. That man had infiltrated every moment of her life, and she thought it might be better to just march out to the blacksmith shop and tell him she liked him.

She clenched her teeth and kept working to get lunch on the table for the cowboys by eleven-thirty. They arrived in shifts, the men and women from the administration meeting coming in first.

Rhodes stepped over to the kitchen and kissed his mother and grandmother hello before snagging a roll at Betsy's protest. She knew Knox wouldn't be there yet, but she couldn't help scanning the group anyway.

Then the work began, and she got busy serving plates of ravioli and getting more butter softened for the rolls. The homestead filled with chatter and laughter, and it made Betsy's heart so happy.

In a lag of serving, she stood back and watched the scene before her. She'd been starting to feel more and more removed from the happenings at the ranch, and she hated that she felt like she was watching the festivities through a pane of glass. She'd knock, but no one heard her.

Then the back door opened again, and a new wave of cowboys entered, Knox with them. Their eyes met, and the temperature in the kitchen increased instantly.

"Behind you," her mother said, and Betsy turned in slow motion. Her mom had another sheet pan of rolls, and Betsy almost reached out to grab it before she remembered it would be hot.

She backed up—right into Knox. She spun, feeling like a ball in a pinball machine, being hit and bounced all over the place.

"Hey," he said playfully, his hand brushing hers. He stepped away a moment later and joined the line. Betsy couldn't get a proper breath, but she moved back into the serving line and got everyone served and on their way to a table.

"Thanks for lunch, Bets," Rhodes said, drawing her into a hug.

"Of course," she said into his chest.

Her older brother released her and asked, "Are you going to stay here and feed me forever?" He laughed and grabbed another roll as someone called his name.

Betsy blinked, sudden emotion welling in her throat and making her eyes hot. Of course she wasn't going to live in the homestead forever. She kept expecting her father to announce his retirement, at which point Rhodes would take over the ranch completely. He already ran the majority of it, and he'd inherit the homestead too. There were other cabins on the property, and Betsy wouldn't be homeless.

Problem was, for her, anywhere but the homestead didn't feel like home at all.

She snapped herself back to the moment, telling herself that it was never good to dwell on what-ifs. She naturally worried about things, and she had to work hard to put things into perspective for herself.

Finally, the last cowboy finished and left, and Betsy started cleaning up from lunch. With the leftovers stored in the fridge and plenty of ravioli in her belly, she retreated to the couch with her phone.

Thanks for lunch, Knox had texted. *I got assigned to the dance committee. Meeting tomorrow night. I'll be at Quinn Valley again tomorrow. Want to ride in with me?*

A smile touched her mouth, and she quickly tapped out a response. *Sure. Thanks.*

And suddenly, tomorrow night couldn't come fast enough. She didn't feel the same annoyance at Rhonda's text that didn't ask when she was available but dictated when and where the meeting would be.

Betsy had worked on the Valentine's Festival in town for twelve years, so Rhonda wasn't the only one with experience. The other woman would definitely have ideas for the dance, but so did Betsy, and she wasn't going to back down this year.

Oh, no. This year, the Valentine's dance would be a masquerade ball, and the eligible men and women of Quinn Valley would have the opportunity to mix and mingle in secret to find their sweetheart.

THE FOLLOWING EVENING, BETSY COULD HARDLY SIT STILL while Jessie plaited her hair. "You're acting weird," her sister said as she hooked another piece of hair and wove it into the rest.

Betsy met her sister's eye in the mirror for just a moment. She felt like she'd been transported back in time two decades, all the jitters of junior high and gearing up to talk to the high school boy she'd had a crush on.

"I am not," she finally said, deciding to keep her secret crush on Knox under her tongue. She hadn't spoken to Georgia, and surprisingly, her sister hadn't been around much. Okay, maybe not surprisingly. She had just made up with Logan a couple of weeks ago, and animal feeding and care in the winter was a full-time job for her sister.

"Don't let Rhonda get to you," Jessie said. "I heard it's her last year chairing the festival."

"Really?" Betsy wasn't sure she believed that.

"Yeah, that's what Renae said when I was there for my foot zoning the other day."

"Hmm." If there was someone who might know, it could be Renae. She saw a lot of people in town, but Betsy tended to wait to believe things until she had first-hand experience or knowledge with them.

"Okay, done," Jessie said, finishing with the elastic at the end of Betsy's braid. "Go show Rhonda that she's not the only one with good ideas." She smiled at Betsy and picked up her flat-iron to curl her hair.

"You going out?" Betsy asked.

"No," Jessie said in a completely false tone.

"So who are you getting dolled up for?"

"No one," she said.

Betsy thought about pushing her, because Jessie was definitely the tomboy of the family and if she was curling her hair…. But she didn't want to have to defend herself and her crush on Knox, so she said, "Okay. Thanks, Jess," and left to get her notes and her winter gear.

Knox knocked on the back door at the same time he entered. She stood in the mudroom, one arm in her coat, and he rushed forward to help her. His hand brushed hers, and time stalled.

"Do you think we have time to stop somewhere for dinner?" he asked. "I'm starving."

Dinner? Was that a date? She buttoned her coat and moved into the kitchen to see the clock on the stove. "Probably not," she said. "Rhonda is a bear if someone is late." She stepped over to the fridge. "I'm sure we have something here. You can eat it on the way in." She dug out some soup, a container of potato casserole, and half a pan of chicken and rice, naming each item as she set it on the counter.

"Did you make all of these?" he asked.

"My mom made the potato casserole. I'd go for that. It's fantastic." She smiled at him, beyond glad when he returned the gesture.

"Hook me up with that then," he said.

She stuck the container in the microwave and got out a fork. "I know where to find you to get this back, Mister." She couldn't believe she was flirting with a fork in her hand, and a rush of foolishness hit her.

But Knox laughed and took the food out of the microwave when it beeped. They left, and he went straight to his truck. "You'll have to drive me all the way back out here," she said, pausing at the bottom of the steps though it was much too cold to dawdle.

"I know," he said, scooping up a bite of potatoes. He stuck them in his mouth and got in the idling truck, leaving her little choice but to do the same.

"It's twenty minutes," she said.

"I know," he repeated. "Now buckle up. The snow melted a little today, and the water is sure to be frozen by now."

The atmosphere in his cab felt charged, and she actually enjoyed it.

"You're a great cook," he said as he got his truck pointed in the right direction.

"Thank you," she said.

"Have you always enjoyed it?"

"You know what? I have. My grandmother taught all of us kids to cook, even Rhodes. My mother was a terrible cook when she married my father, and Granny taught her too."

"Wow," he said.

"Do you cook?" she asked.

He chuckled as he shook his head. "I can heat up hot dogs and make tacos. Stuff like that."

"Oh, we don't make tacos in the Quinn family," she said with false soberness. "That's what Ciran does. Don't you know he makes the best tacos in the world?"

"I did not know that," Knox said. "You'll have to take me sometime."

"He runs the food truck in the winter." She reached over and took the empty container from him, as if they'd known each other for a long time and just knew what the other needed.

"Thanks," he said.

"And sure, we can go get tacos sometime."

"It'll get you off the ranch," he said.

She giggled, horrified at the girlish sound. "You're right."

"So what can I expect at this meeting tonight?" he asked.

"It's usually pretty low-key," she said. "We all sit there while Rhonda tells us what to do. But this year, I'm going to push for a masquerade ball. I've been trying to get one for a few years now."

"Oh, so you volunteer a lot for this?" He cut her a quick look out of the corner of his eye.

"Yeah, for a while now," she said. "Gets me off the ranch." She didn't want to admit that she'd always come to the Valentine's Festival in the hopes that she'd find her own sweetheart.

"You never told me how the cruise was," she said, steering the conversation away from her.

"Oh, it was a big boat and a lot of sunshine," he said.

"You sound like you don't like boats and sunshine," she teased.

"Well, I like one of those things."

"Let me guess: the sunshine."

"I honestly don't know why I live in Idaho," he said. "I could shoe horses in Texas or somewhere warm."

Betsy mentally rejected the idea, but she didn't say anything out loud. "So let's see. You aren't really the monthly poker player kind of guy. You don't like boats. Or winter. What else do I need to know about you?"

"I'm a big fan of hamburgers," he said. "And bacon. And... I'm a pretty simply guy, actually."

"I'm not even sure what color your hair is," she teased. "What with you wearing that cowboy hat all the time."

He swept it off his head and cocked it toward her. "It's brown."

Oh, but it wasn't just brown. It was this gorgeous, dark brown that reminded her of melted chocolate. She licked her lips and looked away while he re-seated his hat. "I think that's called chestnut, actually," she said.

He burst out laughing, and that made Betsy's whole soul warm up. When his chuckles subsided, he asked, "What about you? What do I need to know about you?"

"Oh, I'm an open book," she said. "I cook, I sew, I make jams and jellies." She couldn't help the sarcasm that leaked into her voice.

He looked at her again. "You don't sound happy about that."

"Don't I?" She looked at him, hoping she could tell him something she'd never told anyone. Fear gripped her vocal cords and kept her silent for a few more moments. "Sometimes I get tired of the labels, that's all."

"Labels?"

"Domestic goddess has come up," she said.

"Oh, well, that's not so bad."

"I'm more than my last dish," she said.

Knox looked at her so long, she was sure they'd drive right off the road. "Do people make you feel like you're not?"

"I don't know," she said, because she didn't. "Sometimes I'm just not sure what I'm doing with my life, you know?"

"Yeah," he said quietly as the lights from town came into view. "I know exactly what you mean."

The silence between them was less charged now, and she actually enjoyed the peace in the cab. She'd told him something important to her, and he hadn't brushed it off. Or made her feel stupid for feeling the way she did. Or offered a solution.

He'd simply listened, and she really appreciated that. They pulled into the community center parking lot, and Betsy gathered her folder and her purse.

"All right," she said, facing the doors like she was going to battle. "Let's do this."

CHAPTER SIX

Knox said maybe four words during the meeting. No, he'd said *exactly* four words during the meeting, but they were important ones.

I agree with Betsy.

When they spilled back out into the darkness, she whooped and gave him high five. "I can't believe she agreed. I think you were the linchpin."

"Oh, I doubt that," he said, enjoying the way she was so jazzed that she'd gotten her way and dubbed the theme of the dance as a masquerade.

"No, you were. I think people were divided before you said something."

"I didn't say anything." He opened her door for her and put his hand on her back to guide her into the truck. He really wanted to spend more time with her, and the twenty-minute drive back to the ranch didn't seem like long enough.

But it was the middle of winter, and felt like midnight, and the only thing he could think of was suggesting ice cream.

Or coffee.

She'd offered him coffee at ten-thirty at night last week, and he suddenly realized that she'd wanted to spend more time with him that night.

"Do you want to get some coffee?" he asked.

"Coffee?" Her gaze flew to his. "It's...eight-fifteen."

"So we're agreeing that coffee is just a morning beverage." He chuckled, wishing the sound didn't vibrate with his nerves.

"Not necessarily," she said. "I just don't think Quinn Valley has any coffee shops open this late at night."

"We could go back to my house," he said, the words just materializing in his mouth. "Logan will be there, and he's got these two dogs that track mud all over the place." Knox regretted mentioning his house. It would likely be a mess, and Logan was a better coffee maker than he was anyway.

"What about a sugar cookie and hot chocolate?" she asked as he backed out of the parking spot.

"Where can we go to get that?" His stomach growled for food. Yes, he'd eaten some potatoes, but that wasn't enough for him when he'd been working all day.

"There's a little pastry shop in the strip mall over by the Scentiments shop. I think they're open until nine."

"I thought there was only one bakery in town," he said, stopping at the exit from the lot and turning left.

"There is, but they close at six. This place does quiches, ham and cheese croissants, cream puffs, sugar cookies, flavored sodas, stuff like that. My cousin says the hot chocolate is amazing."

"Let's give it a try." Knox drove down the street, hoping there was something savory still in the shop.

"It's right there." Betsy pointed to the right, and he swung the truck off the road a little too quickly.

"Sorry," he said. Once inside the shop, he saw several savory options, and he ordered three of them. They were the only two people in the shop, and they sat at a flimsy table for two with chairs he wasn't sure would hold his weight.

But the pastry was flaky and warm, cheesy and delicious. She'd ordered sweets and hot chocolate, and she sipped from her mug, leaving a smudge of whipped cream on her nose.

He grinned at her and wiped her face with his napkin while she giggled. Knox hadn't dated anyone for a while, but Betsy was very easy to flirt with, and Knox really wished it was summer and the night was far from over.

As it was, he'd be in a lot of trouble if he didn't get her home and get to bed soon. Yet he lingered over his second croissant, asking her, "So if I was to come to poker night again, what's one thing I could bring that would make you happy?"

"Oh, you nailed it with that seven-layer dip." She grinned at him. "But sometimes a girl just needs a bag of red Starburst."

"Just the red ones?"

"They're the best," she said. "I may or may not have a secret stash of them in the kitchen at the homestead."

Knox laughed again, realizing that he'd been doing that a lot tonight. And he couldn't remember the last time he'd felt so happy. They finished, and he threw their trash in the garbage can by the door while she went out onto the sidewalk. When he joined her, he reached for her hand, relieved and excited when she secured her palm flat against his.

It was a short walk to the truck, but when he got behind the wheel, Betsy had scooted over on the seat to ride right next to him. She slipped her arm through his and laid her head against his bicep as they drove back to the ranch, and Knox's pulse started jumping around like an army of frogs.

"How long have you been a farrier?" she asked.

"Oh, only about a year now," he said. "I went to school in Oklahoma for a bit."

"What did you do before that?"

"Worked on my family's potato farm."

"And you decided that wasn't for you?"

"Nah," he said, lifting his shoulder in a shrug. "My younger brother Alan loves it, and Logan was leaving, so it was easy for me to go too." He liked the gentle pressure of her body next to his, and she was easy to talk to. "So we got a house in town, and we've been making it work."

"But you don't like his dogs."

"I like dogs in general," he said. "But Logan lets his do whatever they want. I really don't like the dogs in the winter."

"So you're a neat freak." She laughed softly, and he smiled into the darkness, glad for good headlights in this rural night.

"Logan thinks so," he said. "Did you ever go to college or anything?"

"Nope," she said. "I took sewing classes from the Bernina on Main Street. And I've taken all the cooking classes from the community center."

"So...what do you do to make money?" Knox wasn't trying to be rude. But didn't she have bills to pay?

"I get paid by the ranch," she said. "I'm the official ranch chef."

"Oh, yeah, that makes sense." And she had somewhere free to live, and tons of vehicles she could use, so her financial obligations probably didn't amount to much. Knox couldn't help the twinge of bitterness that pricked the back of his throat. He and Logan had been scraping and barely getting by for years, and his debt from his many months at farrier school wouldn't be paid off for a long time.

The homestead came into view, and Knox lamented that his time with her was almost up. He pulled to a stop and said, "I won't be back to the ranch until next week."

"That's lame," Betsy said with a giggle. She released his

arm and leaned into him to kiss his cheek. "Thanks for the ride, Knox. And the hot chocolate."

He got out of the truck, and she slid out after him. "What if I said I didn't want to wait until next week to see you?"

They climbed the steps together, this silence full of panic for Knox. Had he given away too many of his feelings too soon?

"Then I'd say you should probably come pick me up for dinner tomorrow night," she said, facing him. She grinned at him, but the smile slipped from her face quickly. "What about Georgia and Logan?" She leaned forward as she spoke, her voice dropping almost to a whisper.

He sighed. "I don't know. Logan made it sound like it wasn't weird."

"You've talked to him about it?"

"Sort of," Knox said. "He called me to come sign up for the Valentine's Festival. I think he figured out I had a crush on you." He sucked in a breath, wishing he could suck in those words at the same time.

Her eyes gleamed under the yellow porch lights, and her smile widened. "I'll talk to Georgia."

"All right." He wasn't sure what to do next, but Betsy opened the door and slipped inside the homestead, so he added, "See you tomorrow."

She ducked her head, and said, "See you then," before closing the door. Though it was easily twenty below zero outside, he floated back to his truck, as warm as if it were the middle of July.

THE FOLLOWING EVENING, KNOX WAS RUNNING LATE. HE'D been out at the dude ranch for-freaking-ever, and he didn't want to get Betsy for their first date smelling like hot steel and horse flesh.

So he'd run home to shower, only to find that Rutabega, one of Logan's dogs, had gotten up on the kitchen counter and dragged everything there onto the floor. The roll of paper towels lay in shreds from the kitchen to the front door, and even up the stairs.

He'd paused inside the door and taken in the room like it was a crime scene and nothing should be disturbed. Then he'd bypassed it all while dictating a text to his brother about the mess at home, and showered in seven minutes.

His text to Betsy had happened at the time he was supposed to be at the ranch, but she'd said it was fine. When he turned onto the ranch property, he almost ran her over.

He hit the brakes and slid a little though his truck had new snow tires. Jumping out, he said, "What are you doing?"

"I was just walking," she said.

"I'm so sorry I'm late," he said, guilt pulling through him. "Sometimes I can't predict what my day will be like." The horses and people he worked with could be temperamental, making a simple job take a long time.

"It's fine," she said, stepping up to him. Her cheeks looked plenty pink in his headlights, and he hurried her over to the passenger door.

"You didn't need to walk."

"Oh, I couldn't go back in the house," she said.

Knox looked at her and paused. "You couldn't?"

"It's too cold to talk with the door open." She flashed him a smile, but it shook on her nearly blue lips.

He closed the door, kicking himself for being so late. He got behind the wheel and turned up the heater fan so it was blowing hard. "So you couldn't go back in the homestead?" He pulled into the driveway of a cabin on the end of the row of three so he could turn around.

"Too many people there," she said. "They'd all ask questions."

"So where do they think you are?"

"I didn't say. I just said I had to go to town."

Knox frowned as he passed Rhodes's cabin and then the one where Betsy's grandparents lived. He eased to a stop at the sign and then turned toward town. "So we're not telling anyone about...." He glanced at her. "Dinner."

"Not yet," she said. "I was thinking we could go over to Riston tonight."

Knox didn't know what to say. He drove, finally deciding that he was old enough to have an adult conversation. "I don't like that we're keeping this a secret."

"I know." Betsy sighed and slid across the seat to sit beside him. She took his hand in hers, and he liked that she wasn't afraid to also show him how she felt. "But we're not really lying."

"We're just not saying anything," he said. "Some would consider that lying."

"My granny said sometimes secrets need to be kept, at least for a little while."

Knox thought about what she'd said. He supposed parents didn't tell their kids about Santa Claus. Or kept secrets for birthdays and special surprises. But no one had gotten hurt by keeping a new bicycle a secret.

"Who are we trying not to hurt?" he asked.

"Georgia," she said. "I just...I don't want her to think I'm crowding her."

"Because Logan is my brother." Knox knew it was a weird situation, no matter what his brother said. Number one, he and Logan were practically identical. Why did Betsy like him and not Logan? Or Georgia like Logan and not him?

"So it's just a little secret," she said. "Until I can talk to Georgia."

"What if she says she thinks it's weird, and she'd rather we didn't see each other?"

Betsy didn't answer, and that didn't provide any comfort for Knox. He let the question hang there for a few minutes, and then he covered it with, "Where are we going in Riston? I only know of the fried chicken place." His mouth watered for the crispy, fried chicken with the sweet, tangy sauce.

"That's great," she said. "I like their sweet potato fries. They're double fried."

Knox wasn't even sure what that meant, but he did know where to go. It was nice to be with Betsy, and she started talking about the chickens she took care of.

"I thought Georgia took care of the farm animals," he said.

"Oh, she does," Betsy said quickly. "But I hatched these chicks myself. Sort of—I don't know. I wanted to prove that I was more than the woman who sewed."

"Well, you cook too," he said, nudging her slightly with his elbow. "And I've heard you make a killer apricot rhubarb jam. Oh, and I believe you're responsible for the gardening around the homestead."

Betsy gave an exaggerated sigh and snuggled into him. "And I raise a trio of chickens," she said.

Knox got the distinct feeling that Betsy needed a reason to be valuable—that she wanted to feel valuable. To who, he wasn't exactly sure. Her family? Herself? Him?

He wasn't sure. But he wanted to find out, and if that meant he had to keep their relationship a secret a little longer, he decided he could do that.

And when he opened the door for her to go into the fried chicken pub, he was even happier they'd made the trip to Riston.

CHAPTER SEVEN

Betsy adjusted her shawl as she quilted, the basement so cold in the winter. She'd even come down that morning before breakfast to turn on the two space heaters down here. How Cami could live down here full-time was beyond Betsy's understanding.

She shivered, but she pulled the needle through the fabric effortlessly. This particular quilt was for Carter and Avery, and she'd put it together in a couple of days and got it on the quilting frame.

She did a lot of sewing and quilting in the winter, because there was no vegetable garden to tend to. No fruit to harvest and make into jams, jellies, or juices. She definitely preferred summer and fall to winter and spring, but she did enjoy quilting. Especially if she could put her aromatherapy oils in the diffuser and turn on some soft music.

Jessie teased her that she was an eighty-year-old woman trapped in a thirty-four-year-old body, and Betsy always laughed with her. So she liked florals better than trendy patterns. And quilting more than surfing the Internet. Didn't mean she wasn't a good person or didn't have value.

Still, Knox's question from over a week ago continued to plague her. *What do you do to make money?*

It was a valid question, and Betsy was well-aware that she was a paid housewife only because Rhodes hadn't found one that would do her job for free.

Yet.

Rhodes hadn't found someone to marry and move into the homestead with *yet*.

But he would, and then Betsy would need to figure out what to do with herself. She had no real employable skills, and she hated that.

So do something about it, she thought, and she determined that as soon as she finished this row of quilting, she was going to do exactly that. She needed to be in town at four this afternoon anyway for a planning meeting for the dance, and she could certainly scope out a few prospects for real jobs before that.

Her fingers ached by the time she finished the row, and as she parked outside the bakery, her head pounded too. There was no NOW HIRING sign in the window. She went inside anyway and asked the girl behind the counter if they needed help.

"I'm so sorry," she said. "But I don't think we do. My uncle runs the shop, and he's only here in the mornings. You could ask him."

Betsy didn't need to go through the humiliation twice, but she nodded.

"I could take your name and number." The girl smiled, and that alleviated some of Betsy's embarrassment. "And he could call you."

"Sure," she said, and she gave the girl the information— and then she bought a chocolate croissant filled with peanut butter mouse and chocolate covered pretzels. As she walked out of the shop and bit into the pastry, she knew she wouldn't be getting a job there. She couldn't make pastries like this.

She sat in the parking lot to eat her treat, her mind revolving around other possibilities. Something she could do from home.

"Catering," she said aloud to her and the car. A warm feeling enveloped her that had nothing to do with the heater pumping to keep her from freezing. She rode the high as she drove over to the community center and sat down with Rhonda and two other people on the dance committee.

She'd known their numbers would dwindle once the real work started, and when Rhonda glanced around with disapproval in her dark eyes, Betsy said, "I think a lot of people have jobs, Rhonda. It's four o'clock in the afternoon."

"So we'll just finalize a couple of things we need to get started on for sure," she said. "And we'll meet again on Saturday."

Betsy bristled that every meeting got to be set by her, according to her schedule. If she'd ask people when they could meet, she'd have more success in getting people to volunteer their time and resources. But Betsy said nothing.

"Invitations," Rhonda said. "We can use the Boy Scouts like we usually do to put flyers on doors a day or two beforehand."

"Do we really need to do that?" Betsy asked. "I feel like we spend a lot of money and time giving out slips of paper to people who don't even need them."

"Who wouldn't need them?" Rhonda asked.

Betsy exchanged a glance with Tia, the woman to her right. "Well," Tia said. "Last year, the entire retirement home got papered, and they were having their own Valentine's Day dance. So it was a waste."

She looked nervous, and Betsy wished she could communicate telepathically so she could let Tia know how much she appreciated her speaking up.

"And one or two days beforehand is too late anyway," Betsy said. "People need to have this on their calendars now."

"I'm sure they do," Rhonda said.

"Then why do we need printed flyers?" Betsy challenged.

Rhonda scratched it off her list. "So no printed flyers. Fine."

"No," Betsy said. "I was just asking a question. I do think we should have it on the town website. And it should be going out in the monthly utility bills. And we should utilize our town social media as well."

Rhonda's head wobbled like one of those dolls, and she looked at Betsy with malice in her expression. "I'm putting you in charge of marketing," she said. "Get as many people there as possible."

"No problem," Betsy said, and Rhonda looked at the next item on her list.

"Food," she said. "We need to hire a caterer that can do something romantic and simple. My ideas were cupcakes, cake pops, sugar cookies, that kind of thing. And our budget isn't very big."

Betsy wanted to blurt out that she was starting a catering business, but she felt like she and Rhonda were the only people talking in the meeting, so she waited for Tia or Kate to say something. Neither one of them did.

"I'm available," she said.

"Available?" Rhonda asked icily.

"I'm doing catering now," she said. "I can definitely do cupcakes, cake pops, and sugar cookies." Her imagination started exploding with pinks, reds, and purples, hearts and flowers and everything Valentine's Day.

"What's your fee?" Rhonda asked.

Betsy thought fast, trying to remember what the budget

for refreshments had been in the past. "Five hundred dollars," she said. "That gets enough refreshments for eight hundred people." And if they had more than that, she'd be extremely surprised.

"You think you can get eight hundred people to come?" Rhonda's eyebrows went up, and Tia's head swung back to Betsy.

She was tired of the back-and-forth. She shrugged. "I don't know. But I can bring that many refreshments." Her stomach dropped to her feet. How in the world could she make enough cake pops and cupcakes for that many people, even with the two ovens in the homestead?

She pushed away her nerves, because she wanted this job. It would be her first catering job, and she wasn't even sure five hundred dollars would cover her costs.

"Okay," Rhonda said. "You're hired. I'll get the contract we use for our vendors."

"Great," Betsy said with false confidence. "What's next?"

Rhonda started talking about decorations, and Betsy sat out of the conversation, glad when Kate stepped up and started offering some ideas.

The meeting ended, and Betsy almost skipped out to her car, already dialing Knox. She wanted to tell someone about the things she'd felt and decided today, and she was a bit surprised that Knox was the only person she wanted to share with.

"Hey," he said, something blowing behind him. "Can I call you back in a couple of minutes? I'm in the fire."

"Yeah, sure," she said, hanging up. She drove almost all the way back to the ranch before her phone rang, and she almost drove off the road again as she reached for it.

"Sorry," Knox said. "Just a bad time."

"How did you answer the phone if you were in the fire?"

"Voice," he said.

"Oh." Betsy's phone probably had those kinds of features, but she didn't know how to use them. "Anyway, I wanted to tell you something exciting."

"Exciting? I'm all ears."

"So I've been thinking a lot about my life, and where I'm going to be once Rhodes takes over the ranch and the homestead." She drew in a deep breath.

"I know you've been concerned about that."

"And when you asked me how I made money, I realized that the ranch is paying me to be a housewife. To cook, clean, quilt, and garden. No one pays for those things."

"Sure they do," he said. "There are lots of landscape companies or private chefs or—"

"Catering," she said over him. "I'm going to do some catering, and not only that, I've already got my first job." Her smile felt like it would crack her face, but she couldn't rein it in. She just felt so good about the ideas she'd had that day.

"Wow," he said. "That is exciting. Who hired you?"

"The Valentine's Festival dance committee," she said. "I bet you're wishing you hadn't missed today's meeting now, aren't you?"

He laughed, the sound just as wonderful over the phone as it was in person. "While I'd have loved to been there when you got the job, no. I'm not even a little bit sorry I missed that meeting."

Betsy laughed as she parked around the side of the homestead. "Anyway, I convinced Rhonda that I could do the refreshments for the dance. Now I just have to figure out how to make that many cookies, cupcakes, and cake pops."

"Well, I'm sure you can rent some kitchen space," he said. "Maybe from a restaurant that isn't open in the morning or something."

"That's a great idea, Knox," she said.

"Well, you don't have to sound so surprised." He chuckled, so she knew he wasn't really offended. "I'm going to be here for another couple of hours. Maybe you'd like to bring out some hot chocolate when you get a sec?"

"Oh, you're here?"

"Yep, out in the blacksmith shop."

"I'll see you in a bit then," she said, watching Georgia cross in front of her and continue toward the back door. "I've got to jet." Their call ended, and she got out of her car quickly. She needed to talk to Georgia so she could take her secret sweetheart out of the shadows—and to the Valentine's Day dance.

"Georgia," she called, almost going down on an icy patch of the sidewalk on the side of the house. Her sister waited at the top of the steps, looking confused.

"Oh, there you are," she said. "That was the weirdest thing." She laughed as Betsy hurried up the steps to her.

"I need to talk to you about something," Betsy said, glancing over Georgia's shoulder to see if anyone was lurking just inside the house. "Come on, let's go inside. It's cold."

Once in the mudroom, with the two of them taking off their scarves and gloves, Betsy said, "Would it...I mean, I like Knox Locke."

Georgia looked at her as she hung her coat, having to try to hit the hook twice before she got it. A slow smile spread her lips. "So Logan was right."

"Yes, all right?" Betsy said. "He was right, but I swear I didn't mean for it to happen. He's just so handsome, and kind, and I like talking to him, and...." She let her voice trail off when Georgia started giggling.

"So are you going to ask him out?" she asked.

"Well, we've sort of been seeing each other on the sly."

Georgia bumped her with her hip, said, "I know," and headed into the kitchen.

Betsy scrambled after her. "You knew?"

"Betsy, you may be able to bluff with your cowboy poker buddies, but I'm your sister." She pulled open the fridge and looked inside. "Are you making dinner?"

"No," she said. "There's leftover meatloaf and chicken cordon bleu casserole in there. I might open a salad." She approached where Georgia still stood at the fridge. "So you're okay if Knox and I go out?"

"I think so," Georgia said. "I mean, it's a little weird, but I don't think it's *that* big of a deal."

Betsy squealed and grabbed onto her younger sister, giving her an awkward side-hug. "Thanks, Georgia. Okay." She released her sister and blew out her breath. "Now, let's put together something to eat and some hot chocolate."

Georgia went around the kitchen island and sat at the bar as if Betsy would serve her. She supposed it was just as easy to put together three plates as two, and then she'd slip out the back door and down to the blacksmith shop, the way she had on Christmas Eve, almost a month ago.

Her heart expanded and warmed as she stirred the milk on the stove, because she was finally going to get to go out in public with her new boyfriend, Knox Locke.

CHAPTER EIGHT

Knox finished the work he needed to do about ten minutes before Betsy pushed through the door, carrying a box in both arms.

"Why didn't you call me?" he asked, jumping off his stool to go help her.

"I'm fine," she said, but she quickly passed the box to him, and it was heavier than she should've been carrying all the way from the homestead. "I brought some leftover casserole, because I figured you hadn't eaten yet. And I threw together a quick salad. And of course, there's the hot chocolate." She plucked a bag of marshmallows out of the bag and ripped into it, taking out a squishy treat and biting into it.

He made a face even as a slip of happiness moved through him. "Gross," he said.

"You don't like marshmallows?" she asked around the mouthful of the gooey treat. She grinned at him, and he shook his head.

"I like them *in* the hot chocolate." He lifted a thermos. "Is this one mine?"

"Either one," she said. "They're the same."

He unscrewed the lid and held it toward her. "Marshmallow me."

She put a couple of marshmallows in his hot chocolate, and he looked back in the box for a spoon. He stirred, steam lifting up past the marshmallows, the heat starting to melt them into his drink.

"This is too hot to drink right now." He set the thermos down on the bench and looked back into the box. "You didn't have to bring dinner." But he sure was grateful, and a rush of affection for her lifted his spirits.

"I talked to Georgia," she said, and he abandoned the food to face her fully.

"You did? And?"

Betsy toyed with the end of her hair, the bag of marshmallows forgotten. "And she said she didn't think it was too weird, me and you seeing each other." She smiled at him, a hint of trepidation in her eyes.

Relief and joy mixed together and spiraled through him. "That's so great." He took a step toward her, not quite thinking rationally. He took her into his arms and held her close, his heartbeat starting to gallop when her arms came up around his neck too.

He pulled back slightly and looked down at her. The temperature in the blacksmith shop was already stifling hot, but the sparks between them felt explosive. Without thinking and without asking, he ducked his head and touched his mouth to hers.

She tasted sweet, like marshmallows, and pure fire roared through his bloodstream now. He kissed her again, this time more than just a touch. She seemed to melt into him, and she kissed him right on back.

Knox hadn't had a girlfriend in a while, and he sure enjoyed his kiss with the beautiful Betsy Quinn.

She giggled, breaking their connection, and he breathed in deep and exhaled heavily, trying to calm his racing pulse.

"So I guess I can ask you to the Valentine's dance now, right?" he asked.

She looked at him with a bit of shock in her expression. "You want to go to the dance together?"

"Well, I'm not dating anyone else." He watched her as she reached past him and into the box, withdrawing a plastic container of food.

She handed it to him and grinned. "I'd love to. You know you have to dress up and wear a mask, right?"

"Shoot." He popped the lid on the container and reached for his spoon. After licking it clean, he stirred the chunks of chicken and ham together, noting the cheesy sauce they were in. "But I guess I can make that work."

"I guess you can," she said, taking her own container and opening it. "It's going to be amazing."

I think you're amazing, he thought, but instead of saying it, he put a bite of casserole into his mouth. He and Betsy spent a half an hour in the blacksmith shop, eating and talking and laughing, and it easily became thirty of the best minutes of his life.

She boxed all the containers and empty thermoses up and lifted the box. "Just a sec," he said, taking the box from her and putting it back on the shelf.

Then he kissed her again.

SOMETHING SMELLED STRANGE WHEN KNOX PULLED UNDER the sign announcing his arrival at Fern Hollow, the dude ranch where he worked a couple of times a week. Sometimes only one day, sometimes more, depending on their needs.

He liked his boss out here, and he'd even considered

coming out for a weekend or so himself. They offered horseback riding excursions, life in real cowboy cabins, chuckwagon dinners, and more.

The real cowboy lifestyle. People loved coming to the country to escape their high-pressured jobs in the city, and while Knox didn't exactly have one of those, he thought he'd still like a weekend away.

And now, maybe Betsy would come with him.

He smiled just thinking about her, despite the foul odor perfuming the air. Quinn Valley had started smelling like sugar and chocolate over the past couple of weeks, and that suited Knox just fine.

As did kissing the baker responsible for making every cowboy within the ranch fences come flocking to the homestead for a taste of her treats. Sometimes he had to text her to come down to the smithy, and sometimes she gave him a quick look and disappeared downstairs. He'd wait a minute or two and follow her, just so they could be alone for a moment, breathe each other in, steal a kiss, and then go about their day.

Knox had never experienced such strong feelings for a woman before, but he sure did like Betsy.

He parked in his usual spot by the stables and got out of the truck. "What is that?" he asked himself, trying to locate the source of the smell. It wasn't the typical smell one would find on a ranch—manure, hay, sometimes even mechanical scents.

This was something rotten. Not quite on the caliber of foul eggs, but very close. He gathered his apron and tools and went inside, where the scent was only slightly less offensive. He found the horse trainer there, and she had a bandana tied around her nose and mouth.

"Wills," he said by way of greeting. "What's going on out here?"

"Oh, something happened with the sewer system," she said, the fabric fluttering slightly around her mouth. "It's awful, ain't it?" She shook her head, and while he couldn't see her mouth, her eyes smiled at him.

"Does the bandana help?" He tied his apron around his waist and walked over to the clipboard hanging on the wall.

"Marginally," she said.

He smiled and glanced at the clipboard. George wrote notes throughout the week, and then Knox knew what to do when he came in. Today, it looked like a few horses had thrown shoes and a few more needed routine work done on their hooves.

He hated winter, but he didn't let it show as he moved down the aisle to the first horse who couldn't seem to keep his shoes on for more than a week. "What's the matter, Vulture?" he asked the horse. "The ground's too hard for you?"

The horse, a beautiful black creature with white markings on his face, came over and snuffled at Knox as if to say, *That's right, Knox. Everything's frozen out there. Didn't you know?*

Oh, Knox knew. He felt the sting of the cold way down in his lungs. Working would help, so he stepped into the stall with the horse and said, "Let's measure you up, then. Get this done."

He wasn't sure if the smell got better or if he just got used to it. No matter what, by the end of the day, he'd accomplished everything on George's list and he didn't feel like he was about to lose his lunch. So, a win.

His phone rang as he loaded up his tools in the back of his truck, and he swiped on the call from Carter Quinn, an organic farmer he worked with from time to time.

"Hey, Carter," he said.

"So it's Cooper again...."

Knox chuckled. "All right."

"I'm not sure where you are or when you can come."

"I'm finishing up at Fern Hollow," he said, closing the tail gate. "I can be out to you in just a few."

"Thank you, Knox." The man sounded so relieved, and Knox understood. Carter loved his horses, and they were almost like members of the family. Cooper was a special one too, and Knox got behind the wheel and turned on the heater before texting Betsy.

Heading out to your cousin's place. Are we still on for a quick dinner? He'd made it down the dirt roads on the dude ranch to the highway before she answered.

I'm so sorry, her text said. *I can't do dinner tonight. I'm up to my elbows in frosting and it's poker night.*

Knox's gut twisted. Poker night. Of course.

"Text Betsy Quinn," he said to his truck.

"Ready to text Betsy Quinn," the truck said back.

"Oh, right, poker night," he said slowly, in a clear voice. "Well, I'll see you later then." He reached over and tapped the send button on the screen in his dashboard and settled in for the drive to Quinn Organics.

He'd never considered himself a jealous man before. Well, maybe a little as a teenager growing up in Logan's perpetual shadow. His brother had never made him feel less than he was, but Knox knew he wasn't as charismatic as his twin.

But something boiled and bubbled in his blood now. He didn't like the fact that Betsy would be spending her evening with four other men, and he wondered what that said about his own feelings for the pretty redheaded Quinn.

Was he in love with her?

He had no idea, and luckily he had a horse to focus on to drive his confusing questions away.

CHAPTER NINE

By the time Betsy cleaned up the kitchen, played poker, and returned to the homestead, she'd been up for nineteen hours straight. Exhaustion made her sag into bed still fully clothed, and she decided she didn't care.

She'd been getting up early to go into the pub to use their kitchen for a couple of hours before Maggie and Bethany kicked her out. There were definite perks to being a Quinn, and the access to a bigger kitchen with ovens that could bake three times as many cupcakes in half the time was one of them.

But wow, four a.m. came really quickly, and Betsy wasn't sure anything should be awake in so much darkness and such chilly conditions.

Her dedication to her new catering business took every spare moment she had, what with designing a logo, a website, and making a price list of dishes she could produce. She's spent hours online looking at other caterers from around the country, and she'd learned that some only did birthday parties. Some did full-course meals. Some cooked in people's homes, and some had industrial kitchens.

It had taken her about a week—and a lot of prayer—before she'd decided she wanted to do something that emulated the ranch that had been in her family for decades. Idaho was full of people doing chuckwagon dinners—heck, there was a dude ranch right here in the valley offering such an experience.

She'd gravitated more toward the Dutch oven dishes she was famous for in the summer. Her peach and cherry cobblers were always a big hit, and she had barbecue chicken recipes and beef short rib pots and even a pork loin she could do in a Dutch oven.

And thus, Cast Iron Catering had been born. It wasn't really in line with the cake pops and sugar cookies she labored over in the mornings, but she decided that didn't matter. She'd have business cards and her website completely ready for booking by the Valentine's Festival, and then people could book her for their family events, weddings, and more.

Just as she was drifting off to sleep, she remembered she'd wanted to invite Knox to church with her this weekend. So she quickly grabbed her phone and sent him a text. Their texting sessions would sometimes go this close to midnight, and sometimes not, so she wasn't sure if he'd be awake right now or not.

But a text came back from him with one word—*Sure*—and Betsy smiled up at the ceiling as she clasped her phone to her chest. She finally fell asleep with Knox's handsome face in her mind.

SUNDAY DAWNED BRIGHT AND EARLY, BUT AT LEAST IT wasn't four a.m. The pub didn't open until later on Sundays, and it would've been a great day to get a few extra hours of practice in. But Betsy reasoned that the Good Lord had taken a day off each week, and she could too.

She put three racks of baby back pork ribs in the Crock pot before church, and then stood in the bathroom with Jessie and Georgia, worrying over her hair.

"Why are you so fidgety?" Jessie finally asked when Betsy had elbowed her for a third time.

"Knox is coming to church today," she said, flat ironing another lock of hair that refused to curl as much as the pieces around it. "Why is my hair doing this today?" Frustration seeped through her, and she let Jessie take the iron from her.

"So you like him," she said.

Betsy's eyes met Georgia's in the mirror, and Georgia wore an intense look in hers. "I mean, yes," Betsy said, her voice smaller than she'd like. She was older than Georgia and the other sisters, but sometimes she felt so insignificant compared to them.

Georgia smiled at her and finished her mascara. "That's because those Locke men are amazing." She giggled and left the bathroom as Jessie called after her.

"Don't they have another brother?"

Georgia didn't answer, but Betsy said, "Yes, his name is Alan. He's taking over the potato farm."

"Hmm," Jessie said, finally getting the errant curl to work. "There you go, sis."

"Who would you invite to church?" she asked, remembering how Jessie, who usually didn't care if her hair was in a perpetual ponytail, had curled her hair a few weeks ago.

Her face colored slightly, making her freckles more prominent. "Oh, no one."

"Mm hm," Betsy said, glancing out the door and then pushing it closed with her foot. "You can tell me, you know. I mean, I had to talk to Georgia about dating her boyfriend's twin. That was hard."

"He works for us," Jessie said in a whisper.

"So did Logan and Knox," Betsy stage-whispered back.

"Logan did not work for us," Jessie argued. "Georgia fake-hired him. And Knox, well, I guess he does work for us, but it's not full-time, and it just feels different."

"And look at all of us now." Betsy gave her sister a *so there* look. Not that she and Knox were as serious as Georgia and Logan. They'd started talking about buying a ranch together and Georgia even went to a counselor now to deal with some of her past feelings from an ex-boyfriend. She wanted to be with Logan, and everyone in the family was expecting a proposal in the future.

"He has a girlfriend." She pressed her lips together and shook her head. "I'm not saying."

"All right," Betsy said, mentally going through each man who worked on the ranch. After all, she knew them all, fed them all. "But you can tell me, and then maybe I can help you get a date with him."

"He has a girlfriend," Jessie repeated, opening the door and exiting the bathroom. She paused and stuck her head back in. "But thanks, Bets."

She stayed in the bathroom for another moment, still trying to find the right man that Jessie would have a crush on.

"Flynn," she said. He had a new girlfriend every time they met to play poker, though. Surely Jessie knew that. Betsy would just tell her, let her know that Flynn Hollister would *definitely* go out with her if she asked.

The conversation had stilled her nerves for a few minutes, but with every turn of the wheels that took them closer to the little white church on the outskirts of town pushed her closer to throwing up.

She'd never invited a man to church before, and Knox would have to be paraded in front of the whole Quinn family. Well, at least hers. And Granny and Gramps, and all of

Granny's friends...oh, yes. Several of them would say something, and Betsy was sure she'd be the topic of conversation at Granny's mid-week luncheon with her white-haired friends.

I'm here, Knox's text came in as Jessie turned the truck carrying her and all the sisters into the church parking lot.

Just parking, she sent back, wondering if she'd worn the wrong thing. It was winter, so it was normal to wear all black like you were attending a funeral. Right?

She walked toward the building with her sisters, all three of them chattering like they didn't have a care in the world. Betsy felt removed from them, behind that glass window again. And then she saw Knox standing on the sidewalk, waiting for her.

He wore a pair of black slacks, those cowboy boots that she suspected were permanently glued to his feet, a black leather jacket with a white shirt peeking out, and his gray cowboy hat.

Everything inside Betsy settled into its normal rhythm, and when Knox smiled at her, fireworks popped through her system. "Ladies," he said to her sisters with a quick nod of his hat. They twittered at him and walked on by. "And wow," he said, scanning her from her curls to her heels. "Don't you look beautiful?"

He swept her into his arms, making her feel cherished and safe, and kissed her temple. He adjusted his hat, took her hand, and faced the church. "I haven't been to church in a while," he admitted, and she heard the undercurrent of nerves in his voice.

"Well, it's not too hard," she said. "You just sit there. Come on." Might as well get it over with. Show him off to everyone in town. After all, their relationship wasn't a secret anymore.

❄

"YES, MAUDE," BETSY SAID AFTER CHURCH, HER grandmother's Wednesday brunch club all gathered around. She swept them with a single gaze. "Knox is my boyfriend."

All the old ladies looked at him now, and he had the decency to blush. His hand in hers tightened, a silent signal for her to get him out of there.

"We have to go," she said. "Sorry. I'm in charge of lunch at the homestead today." Every Sabbath, but surely Granny's friends knew that.

"And Georgia's dating your brother, right?" Betty practically yelled, and sure enough, when Betsy checked, she didn't see any hearing aids in Betty's ears.

"That's right," Knox said, squirming a little beside her.

"Well, what do you know," Ruby said, her voice full of surprise. "A set of twins dating a set of sisters. You don't see that every day."

"Oh, you see it all the time," Granny said, shooing the other women toward the exit. "Come on, girls. I can't stand on this incline in my heels."

"Oh, you and your heels, Gertie," Nellie said as she inched away from Knox and Betsy. "Why don't you just wear flats like the rest of us?"

"My great-granddaughter dated one brother, broke up with him, and then went out with another," Betty screeched.

"Is that so?" Ruby asked. "Well, I'll be. I guess I should've looked at Darrel's brothers before I settled for him." That got the women laughing, but Betsy knew Ruby loved her husband.

They moved out of the chapel ahead of Betsy and Knox, who seemed rooted to the spot.

"So," she said, gently tugging him to get him moving up

the inclined aisle to the back of the chapel too. "Besides that little attack there, what did you think of church?"

"You're right," he said. "It's a lot of sitting."

She giggled, and she'd been slightly more keyed up than normal, which made listening to the sermon a bit hard. Fine, she'd barely heard a word. But she had always liked coming to church. At the very least, it was an hour away from the ranch.

Her sisters loitered in the lobby, and Betsy realized with a flash that she should've sent them on home without her. "Oh, you guys could've gone. I think I'll ride out with Knox." She turned and looked up at him. "You are coming to lunch this afternoon, right?"

"Is lunch part of church?"

"Of course."

"Then, sure. I agreed to come to church."

"Betsy made ribs," Jessie said. "You definitely want to come."

"And maybe you should stop by and get Logan, then," Georgia said. "He won't have left yet, and I invited him too."

Betsy looked at Cami and Jessie, a wicked thought forming in her mind. "Who else wants to invite someone?" she asked.

Cami rolled her eyes and headed for the door. "I'm driving home," she said.

Jessie gave Betsy a pointed look and said, "Look who's acting like Granny now," before she followed Cami.

Georgia just laughed on her way out the door. When Betsy turned back to Knox, he wore a confused look on his face.

"Granny?"

"Oh, my grandmother and her friends have a knack for setting people up," she said. "It's nothing."

"Did they set us up?"

"No," Betsy said slowly. "But it was Granny who suggested

that it was okay to keep some things secret for a while. She caught me when I went out to wish you Merry Christmas."

Knox chuckled and ducked his head against the wind as they moved into the Idaho winter. "So you've had a crush on me for a long time."

"Oh, please," she said. "Like you didn't like me for my cooking."

"Hey," he said a bit defensively. "Can I help it if those were the best ham sandwiches I've ever put in my mouth?"

She laughed, her joy fuller today than it had been in...well, ever. She rode right beside Knox as he drove over to his house, and it wasn't until he'd pulled into the driveway that she realized she was at *his house*.

"You wanna come in?" he asked.

"Definitely."

CHAPTER TEN

Knox tried not to feel nervous about having Betsy—domestic goddess Betsy, who ran the homestead on the ranch—walking toward his house. But the two-story home hadn't had a female touch in years, and he was sure it would be noticeable to a woman like Betsy.

They entered through the front door to find Logan asleep on the couch in the living room, a dog sprawled out on either side of him. Knox practically slammed the door, which caused Mortie to lift his head and sigh. Ruta didn't even move, and Logan snored on.

"He's been really busy with the addition on the library," Knox said. "Apparently, they have to have it done by April first, or they lose some sort of grant." He nudged his brother's shoulder. "Logan. Wake up, bro."

Logan snorted and shifted, his eyes coming open one millimeter at a time. "Oh, hey," he said when he was awake enough to see Knox. "Betsy." He scrambled up, dislodging the dogs, one of which gave another big sigh.

"You're riding out with us to the ranch," Knox said.

"Georgia said she invited you, and it makes no sense for us both to drive out there."

"Sounds great." He yawned and scrubbed his hands through his hair. "I suppose I should shower first. Do I have time for that?"

Knox looked at Betsy, who looked half horrified and half nonchalant. When she didn't say anything, Knox said, "Sure. Make it fast. I think Betsy is in charge of lunch."

"I mean, kind of," she said, but Knox didn't buy it.

"You put in ribs, right?"

"Yeah, but I just have to slather barbecue sauce on them and stick them under the broiler. It takes five minutes." She wandered further into the house, almost entering the kitchen. "Jessie will make the mashed potatoes, and Georgia can slice a roll. I'll text them."

She pulled out her phone while Knox stepped past her and into the kitchen. At least there were no paw prints, no remnants of something the dogs had shredded, and no dirty dishes. So Logan had done something besides lie on the couch and sleep.

"You want something to drink?" he asked, nervous for a reason he couldn't name.

"I'm okay." She glanced up from her phone. "This is a nice place."

"Yeah? There's a den behind the stairs there. A bathroom. Logan and I have bedrooms upstairs."

She trailed her fingers along the countertop and turned to beam at him. "I like it."

"I'd think you'd be accustomed to something much bigger."

"Sometimes the homestead is a little too big, you know?"

No, Knox did not know. But he nodded as if he did. "Are you going to do the baking for the dance at the pub? Or did you decide that the two kitchens at the homestead would work?"

"I'm going to do the cupcakes at the homestead that morning and afternoon," she said, and Knox thought of the sheets and sheets of plans she'd shown him last week. He'd teased her and threatened to throw them in the fire in his shop, but that was only to get her to step into his arms so he could kiss her.

"And I'm going to do the sugar cookies at the pub early-early in the morning on the day of the dance."

"I told you I'd come help."

"I'm okay." She smiled at him and moved over to look at the slips of paper he and Logan kept tacked to their cork board. For some reason, it felt really personal to have her looking at his things, but he didn't move from in front of the fridge.

"How's the stage coming?"

"Oh, I left it to Logan. He thinks I'm good with a hammer, but only if I'm looking at a hoof." He smiled and got a soda out of the fridge, noticing that the shower upstairs had turned off. So Logan would be ready soon. For some reason, Knox wanted to leave. He felt more comfortable with Betsy when they were out on the ranch, and he wondered what that meant. Why he felt like that. And if he'd get over it.

"What about the dance floor?" Betsy asked, coming closer to him.

"I don't know," he said.

"Knox, you're on the committee."

"I've been to a few meetings," he said, a sting pinching in his chest. "I never get anything to do, so I don't see why I even need to go anymore." He didn't mind sitting beside Betsy and watching her get fired up at everything Rhonda said.

He could see that Rhonda was a bit annoying, but she

didn't rub him the wrong way the way she obviously did Betsy.

"I'm sure Logan will take care of it," he said next, because he didn't like the critical way Betsy was watching him.

"I'll take care of what?" Logan asked, thundering down the last few steps.

"The stage and the dance floor," Betsy said, turning away from Knox, her expression stormy.

"Oh, yeah," Logan said, yanking the fridge open and taking out a soda too. "The stage is done. The dance floor is in the den there." He nodded toward the room behind the stairs, and Knox had no idea the dance floor was there. "Are we going?"

"Yes," Knox said quickly. "We're going."

"Let me let the dogs out," he said. "I'll meet you in the truck." If he realized there was some new tension between Knox and Betsy, he didn't act like it. But Knox went back into the living room and out the front door, wishing he didn't feel like Betsy had just treated him like a petulant toddler.

"We have four hundred people who say they're coming to the dance," she said after she got into the truck and slid over to the middle spot on the bench seat.

"That's great," he said, perhaps a slip of sarcasm coloring the words.

Betsy looked at him, and the weight of her gaze was more than Knox could shoulder. He was drawn to look at her despite not wanting to.

"Are you upset?" She searched his face, her eyes earnest.

"A little," he admitted.

A smile touched her mouth. "Wow. I didn't think that was possible."

Knox scoffed and looked out the window, wishing it didn't take Logan's dogs quite so long to take care of their business. "It's possible," he said.

"You're just so calm and cool and collected," Betsy said, touching his arm.

He looked at her fingers and then her, softening toward her. "Yeah, well, you sort of acted like I'd fallen down on a job in there."

"Because of the dance floor?"

"Yeah," he said.

"And that upset you?"

"Yes," he said.

She cocked her head. "Why?"

He considered her for a moment. "Because not everyone is as perfect as you." As soon as he said it, he wished he could take the words back.

She flinched like he'd thrown ice water in her face, and he watched her crumple but try to hide it. She looked away and whispered, "I'm not perfect," just as Logan came jogging from the backyard.

Knox didn't have time to say anything else before Logan got in the truck with a loud sigh. "Sorry. Mortie was very indecisive."

Knox just put the truck in reverse and backed out of the driveway. He loved the roads in Quinn Valley, where only the main ones had lines on them and it looked like God had poured asphalt out of a bucket in straight lines to make a grid.

Lawns and dirt went right up to the road, and in the winter, people piled snow wherever it would go.

"So what's for lunch, Betsy?" Logan asked easily, clearly oblivious to the atmosphere in the cab.

"Ribs," she said. "Mashed potatoes." She continued to talk about lunch and the ranch, and Knox sat there like a statue, only moving when he needed to turn or switch on the windshield wipers as the snow started to flurry through the sky.

At the homestead, Betsy blended into the chaos in the

kitchen, easily stealing away from Knox and putting distance between them. He migrated over to Rhodes, who sat at the kitchen table with his father and grandfather. At first, Knox thought he might be interrupting, but Rhodes smiled heartily at him and said, "We were just talking about you."

Not that he felt better about that. "Oh?"

"Yeah." Rhodes tapped the table next to him, and Knox sat down. "Gramps, this is the man I was telling you about. He's dating Betsy."

"Oh, you're a brave one," the older man said with a hoarse chuckle following.

"Betsy's a good woman," Rhodes's father said, and Knox had no idea what he should say.

"Of course she is," Gramps said, and Knox realized he wasn't part of the conversation at all. "I was just saying she's full of fire."

"Is she?"

"I've seen her in a dance committee meeting," Knox said, unsure of where the words came from. "And she was full of fire."

"That's because she doesn't like Rhonda Drexel," Rhodes said.

"Why is that?" his father asked.

Rhodes glanced into the kitchen, where the majority of the women worked. Logan sat at the counter, and he said something that caused an uproar of laughter. Knox turned back to the men at the table at the same time Rhodes did.

"Oh, Rhonda stole Betsy's boyfriend in high school. She's never quite gotten over it."

"Lunch time," Betsy herself announced, and Knox stood up with everyone else besides Gramps. She went through the food as if everyone in the homestead were blind, and Knox fell to the back of the line, having always noticed that Betsy waited until the very end to get herself any food.

He edged over to her, craving the feel of her hand in his, but he wasn't sure if he was allowed. "I'm sorry," he said out of the corner of his mouth. "I didn't mean to make it sound like you being perfect was a bad thing."

"Nobody's perfect," she said, keeping her eyes on the people moving through line. There were substantially less people than what she fed for lunch, yet she watched them like a hawk.

"Maybe I sometimes, compared to you, just feel...inadequate."

Betsy faced him then, and he knew he'd said something important to draw her away from lunch. "I have never thought that about you."

He did take her hand then, squeezing it. "Thanks, Betsy." He pressed his lips to her temple and joined the line. Maybe he could salvage this day with ribs and mashed potatoes.

AFTER LUNCH, HE FOUND HIMSELF OUT ON THE RANCH with Betsy, watching her toss feed to the chickens. "See, that one's named Henrietta," she said, nodding to a black hen. "And this one's called Chuckles." She beamed down at him and cocked her head. "See how he chuckles all the time."

Knox listened, and he could hear the chicken making some clucky warbling sounds in the back of his throat even as he ate. The simplicity of the creature made him smile, and the fact that Betsy loved these chickens also warmed his heart.

"How's the catering coming?" he asked, taking a handful of feed from her bucket and tossing it to the third chicken, who loitered in the corner.

"Bennie," she called to him. "Come eat, boy."

Knox chuckled at the way she talked to the fowl like it

was a dog, and the chicken in the corner didn't move. He wore a wild look in his eye, and Knox wondered if the animal was sick. Betsy didn't answer his question, and she edged away from him, clucking to her precious chickens.

So the catering business wasn't going well. Last she'd told him, she was working on her menu, prices, and website.

He decided he didn't want to let her put the distance between them, so he trailed after her and asked, "Do you still want to be a caterer, Bets?"

CHAPTER ELEVEN

*B*etsy shrugged her shoulders, sudden emotion at Knox's question rising through her throat and stifling her voice.

"What's wrong?" he asked, brushing his fingers along hers. He portrayed compassion and clear concern in his question, and she didn't think he'd let her get away with ignoring him a second time.

"I'm not sure I want to be a caterer," she said. "I mean, I want to do *some*thing. And I've spent a ton of time on the plans and website over the past couple of weeks." She tipped the bucket and dropped the last of the chicken feed onto the ground.

The sun shone brightly, providing some warmth to the day though it was mostly a mirage.

"So I don't know." She turned toward him, barely meeting his eye as she headed back to the shed where the chicken supplies were kept.

"What do you want to do?" Knox asked, taking her hand and strolling like it was summertime. "If you could have anything you wanted, do anything, live anywhere, what would it be?"

Betsy studied the ground as she walked. "I'm afraid to say."

"You can tell me," he said gently. "Isn't that what we're doing? Sharing important things about ourselves? What we really want?"

That was exactly what Betsy wanted, but she heard the incredulity in his voice when he asked her what she did to make money, all those weeks ago.

"I'm still figuring it out," she said. "I'll let you know when I do."

"Maybe I could help you."

Maybe he could, but she still didn't want to tell him that she wanted his brother to build her a house near the entrance of the ranch so she could quilt, bake, and garden to her heart's content. Would he support her...doing nothing?

It's not nothing, she told herself. Her mother had never had a job. She'd raised the kids, made sure breakfast was eaten before school, homework and piano lessons done afterward, and now she claimed to be preparing herself for grandparenthood.

She and Knox made it back to the homestead, and she paused on the front porch and tipped up on her toes. "I'm sorry I upset you earlier today."

"I know," he murmured just before kissing her. Betsy felt herself falling, falling, falling. She held onto his shoulders, and touched his hair, and cradled his face in her palms until someone opened the front door and caused them to jump apart.

"Granny wants to play a game," Jessie said, poking her head out. "And all the blinds are open, just so you know." She gave them a look that said *stop making out on the porch where we can all see*, and she ducked back inside.

"You up for a game with my family?" she asked.

"Is it bad?" Knox asked.

"Oh, Rhodes is a cheater and will defend himself to the death. My mom usually gets upset about halfway through and leaves to go make cookies. And Jessie wins everything."

"So that's why you don't invite her to poker night," he said, a smile on his face.

"Oh, there's so many reasons she can't come to poker night," Betsy said, reaching for the doorknob.

"Oh?" Knox moved to follow her. "What's another one?"

"All the cowboys love her," she said, pushing open the door and going inside the house. A rush of warmth greeted her, and she sighed into it, glad there would be more people to distract Knox's attention from her and her lowly dreams to be a homemaker and mother.

As she scanned the crowd, she decided right then and there to invite Jessie to poker night. Then she'd see Flynn and Betsy would know if he was the one her sister was crushing on.

ANOTHER WEEK WENT BY, AND THEY WERE ANOTHER WEEK closer to Valentine's Day. She'd stopped practicing the baking in the morning, and she hadn't worked on Cast Iron Catering for another minute.

With just over a week to go until the fourteenth, Wednesday morning found her walking down the long road from the homestead to her grandparent's home near the entrance of the ranch.

Granny's friends would be coming over for lunch in a few hours, and she'd asked Betsy to come help her make a brunch that wouldn't be forgotten. Specifically, she wanted Betsy's famous ham and egg breakfast sliders. They were popular on

Christmas morning, as they could be made ahead of time. Or when Rhodes wanted to have real food at a tailgate party for the Superbowl. Or New Year's Day.

Betsy hadn't made them for any of those events this year, and Granny would be pairing the sliders with her special fruit salad, peach punch, and her lemon poppy seed muffins.

In fact, Betsy could smell the citrusy goodness when she was still a block or two away from her granny's cabin. She'd learned to bake the muffins as one of the first recipes Granny had trusted her to do solo.

"Granny," she said as she entered the cabin, her cheeks tingling as they warmed up.

"Come in, come in," Granny said from the kitchen. She'd already put her serving platters and trays on the dining room table, along with five place settings for her and her friends. "I'm ready to learn your ways."

She smiled and accepted a hug from Betsy, holding her at arm's length and looking right into her face. Betsy used to hate it when Granny did this, as if she could see right into Betsy's soul.

Of course, that was back when Betsy did things she didn't want her grandmother to know about, like sneaking off with a boy or skipping class to go to lunch with her friends.

"You and Knox are getting along okay," Granny finally decreed, and Betsy smiled at her.

"Most of the time," she said.

She released her and bent to look at the muffins through the glass in the front of the oven. "What's holding you back?"

Granny was a safe person, and Betsy had always been able to talk to her. "Has it ever occurred to you that I don't really do anything around the ranch?"

Her grandmother straightened and looked Betsy right in the eye. "What?"

"I make lunch sometimes," she said with a sigh, turning

away from her grandmother's sharp eyes. "Is that really what my life is going to be?"

Gramps came in from outside, stamping his feet and going, "Whoo-ee! It's freezing out there, but the well is as good as ever." He stepped into the kitchen, shaking his hat in one hand. "Oh, morning, Betsy."

"What are you doing today?" Betsy asked, opening a drawer and putting on an apron.

"Oh, Dusty is coming to get me and take me to the movies."

"He likes to flirt with the girl who sells popcorn there," Granny said as if she was mentioning that it would snow later.

"Of course he does," Betsy said dryly. It was no family—or town—secret that Dusty was a huge flirt.

"Betsy was just telling me that she wants to follow in my footsteps and be a professional homemaker."

Betsy froze, ice filling her chest. "Granny, I didn't mean—"

"I know exactly what you meant," she said, pulling two cartons of eggs out of the fridge. "Women these days are so progressive, but you know, there's nothing wrong with being a homemaker. And you're very, very good at it. Knox would be a very lucky man to have you waiting for him at home."

"Just like I have been to have you waiting for me at home all these years," Gramps said, giving Granny a quick squeeze. He faced Betsy, a wrinkly grin on his face. "She does kick me out every Wednesday, but I still love her."

Betsy laughed with her grandfather while Granny rolled her eyes and scoffed. "Do I have to wait for him?" she asked. "I mean, you didn't just sit around and wait for Gramps to come in off the ranch, did you?"

"Heavens, no," Granny said, pointing to the two bags of rolls on the counter. Betsy reached for them, wondering if she really had to be more, do more, be something, do something, to be a valuable part of her family. Or valuable to society. Or to Knox.

"Sometimes, you want him waiting for you, you know?" Granny purred in the back of her throat, and Betsy laughed again. "Now, let's get started on these sliders. Gramps won't go until he gets some breakfast."

Betsy started instructing about the layers, and the cheese, ham, and scrambled eggs came together quickly. It was really quite an easy dish, and her mind was allowed to wander toward the future she wanted for herself.

No money restrictions. No roadblocks at all.

In it, she saw herself feeding people and making them happy—basically what she did now.

She saw a home of her own here on the ranch—which seemed impossible.

She saw her and Knox—which infused fear right into her bloodstream. Would he want her if she didn't have grand aspirations for herself or a career?

BETSY MIXED HER DRY INGREDIENTS WITH HER WET, THE kitchen in the pub quite chilly this early in the morning. She was going through one last practice run with the sugar cookies, and she actually enjoyed the date with herself, the stainless steel work benches, and the dough.

She rolled and cut, each cookie a wonderful four-inch tall heart that would puff and then crinkle along the edges. She hoped. She got the first four sheet pans in the fridge to chill while she used the giant mixing bowl to stir up another batch of dough.

By the time Bethany showed up at seven to start her daily prep for the pub, Betsy had one hundred and ninety-two cookies and the cream cheese frosting to go with them. She'd made this many cookies three previous times, and she boxed up twenty to take out to the ranch.

The rest she'd take to the bakery on her way back to Quinn Valley.

"Want a cookie?" Betsy tipped the plastic container toward Bethany, who plucked four out.

"Thanks, Betsy. You all ready for the big day?"

Betsy drew a deep breath and blew it out. "I sure hope so. I am so done getting up this early." She flashed a grin at the chef who'd married her cousin, Ryder. Meeting a Quinn honestly wasn't hard to do. If Betsy threw a rock, she'd hit a Quinn, and that was saying something as throwing certainly wasn't her strong suit.

Bethany laughed. "You get used to it."

"Well, at this point, I'll be glad when this dance is over."

"Really? You seem to love it." Bethany pulled a binder out and flipped it open, glancing through it. To Betsy, it looked like recipes or a list of menu items, and Bethany tied an apron on while Betsy started taking her huge bin of cookies out to the car.

Thankfully, Marge at the bakery had been paying Betsy for the cookies, so she'd been able to replace the ingredients she'd been buying.

"Betsy," Marge said when she came stumbling through the bakery doors. "Let me help you." But the older woman couldn't really do much except clear some counter space. Betsy slid the cookies onto the counter with a huff and wiped her hair off her forehead.

"There's about a hundred and seventy here this morning," she said.

Marge punched a button on her cash register, and the till popped open. "I can't wait to see these all displayed at the dance." She counted out some twenties and handed them to Betsy.

"Thanks." She folded the money and tucked it in her pocket. "I'm still good to use your trays and stands, right?"

"Of course, dear. I'll meet you at the community center about an hour before it starts."

"Oh, I can come get them from you."

Marge laughed and shook her head. "Nope. I'll have Culver load them in our delivery van. We'll see you there." She looked over Betsy's shoulder as the bell rang and another customer came in.

Betsy left the bakery, glad she hadn't had to be there at three o'clock in the morning and then act happy to see people when they came in. Betsy needed a nap, stat.

A few hours later, her bladder woke her, and she stumbled out of her bedroom only to see Knox standing there. He wore his regular farrier clothes, but the apron had been left somewhere else.

"There you are," he said, holding his position at the end of the hall. She needed to go right to the bathroom, but Knox was on her left, and she was torn. "Taking a nap?"

She ran her hand through her messy hair and tried to laugh. But embarrassment squirreled through her. "Yeah, I was up early this morning."

"Aren't we all?" He cocked his head at her, that smile seemingly stuck in place. "Well, I won't interrupt you. Must be quite the life, napping before ten a.m."

Betsy felt like someone had poured dry ice down her throat, and it cooled and froze everything it touched. Her vocal cords. Her lungs. Her stomach. She could simply stare at Knox, and blink.

Must be quite the life, napping before ten a.m.

He had no idea that she'd been up late with Georgia as her sister lamented the ill health of one of her potbellied pigs, then up early to get into the pub to practice the cookies. She didn't need to justify a nap to him, or to anyone.

She retreated inside herself, folded her arms, and forced a laugh out of her mouth. She'd known for about a week how she'd answer his question about what she wanted her future to look like, but she hadn't told him.

"I'll be right back," she said and started toward the bathroom.

"I was just leaving," he called after her, and she raised her hand in a farewell wave. Inside the bathroom, she closed and locked the door, her fingers trembling. She pressed her palms flat against the vanity and looked at herself in the mirror.

She was a mess, with half of her hair matted on one side and her skin so pale, she could've passed for a zombie.

"Shouldn't matter," she said to her reflection. Knox should be able to see her in any condition and find her beautiful. Did he?

She had no idea.

What she did know made her heart ache and tears prick the backs of her eyes. She didn't want to tell him why she was taking a nap. Didn't want to include him in the good news that every single cookie had come out perfectly. Didn't want to share with him that the future she'd seen for herself involved him.

Because now, she wasn't so sure it did.

CHAPTER TWELVE

Knox worked in the blacksmith shop, able to juggle hot pieces with his gloves easily. He'd waited in the homestead for at least ten minutes for Betsy to come out of the bathroom, but she never had.

He'd texted her that he hoped he could come up to the homestead for lunch, but she hadn't responded yet. Maybe she was sick. She hadn't looked great coming out of her bedroom, and a pang of concern ran through him.

His phone finally chimed, and he glanced at it, expecting to see a *Sure, come up for lunch* message from Betsy.

Instead he saw, *I don't think so, Knox.*

The text was from Betsy, but the response didn't make sense. He set aside his tools, peeled off his gloves, and picked up the phone.

"I don't think so?" Instead of sending texts back and forth for the next thirty minutes, he decided to call her. She didn't pick up, but he got a text from her while the line was ringing.

So she didn't want to talk to him. Knox may not have had a lot of experience with women, but the messages she was sending were loud and clear.

The physical one she'd sent said, *I know the answer to your question now. I know what I want my future to be like, and you're not in it.*

The breath left his body, and he almost dropped his phone just as another text came in.

I'm sorry, Knox.

Her apology seared his eyes, and he didn't know what to do. If he splashed liquid metal where it shouldn't go, he knew how to fix it. Reform it. Reheat it. But this pain firing through him couldn't be quenched with a bucket of water at the end of the bench.

It burned a path through his body, and he seized onto the one thing he thought he could use to get her to change her mind. *What about the dance? You asked me to go with you.*

He'd pressed his slacks and ordered a black dress shirt and a mask to make him look like the Phantom of the Opera. It wouldn't be original, but he didn't care. It was as close to masked as he was going to get, and though Betsy had asked him what his plans were, he'd steadfastly refused to tell her.

I had to be there for the refreshments, she texted. *I won't have time to dance anyway.*

What did I do? he asked next, because he had to have done something. Sure, things had been a little strained over the past couple of weeks, but they'd talked them through. Held hands. Went to church together.

Nothing, she sent back.

"Nothing?" he scoffed, the scent of fire and ash choking him. He couldn't stay here right now, and he hurried to quench the flames and get out of the shop. He marched right back to the homestead, the desire to get a real answer driving him right up the steps and into the kitchen. Betsy sat at the counter with a bowl of cereal in front of her, and she glanced up with surprise when he entered.

"Nothing?" he repeated, holding up his phone. "I don't believe that."

She leaned away from her cereal, her hair less matted now though she still wore her pajamas. Several long moments passed before she said, "I don't want to be a caterer. I don't want to have my own bakery. I don't have aspirations to do anything but what I'm currently doing."

"Okay," he said.

"No," she shot back. "It's not okay. You want me to be more than I am, and for a while there, I thought I did too. But I don't." She picked up her bowl, slid off the barstool, and walked over to the sink.

He tracked her every move, wondering when he'd ever given her the impression that she needed to be more than she already was.

"I want to quilt during the day. Or nap. Raise kids. Check homework. Give piano lessons after school." She wiped her eyes, but her voice remained strong. "The only difference between the future I want and the life I have now is that I need my own house to do it. But I want it to be here on the ranch. I'm going to talk to Rhodes about it today."

Knox had no idea what to say, so he didn't say anything.

Betsy lifted her chin. "And I didn't see you in my future."

"So you're going to have a family with someone else?" Knox couldn't believe he'd asked that. They'd been dating for five weeks, and they hadn't quite talked about children or marriage or serious things yet.

"I don't know," she said, her chin wobbling. "Please, you're making this harder than it needs to be."

"Betsy," he said, feeling very much like he was about to lose control of his emotions. His throat narrowed and closed, and he couldn't say anything else. The door behind him opened, and Jessie came inside, stamping the snow from her feet.

"Oh, hey, Knox," she said edging past him. As soon as she saw Betsy, she froze. "What's going on?"

"Nothing," Betsy said, her voice much too high. "Knox was just leaving." She stared at him, begging him with those beautiful eyes to just go.

So he did.

THAT NIGHT, KNOX STOOD AT HIS BEDROOM WINDOW AND gazed out into the night. It was Thursday night. Second one of the month, which meant Betsy would be in that blasted east stable, playing poker with four other men.

He knew where to find her. He could go see her, demand she tell him what he'd done so he could fix it.

But he didn't move a muscle, and he knew he wouldn't be driving back out to Quinn Valley Ranch tonight. Or tomorrow, as he had work at Fern Hollow. His mind flowed over the weekend events, and how everything would be altered now that Betsy had cut herself out of his life.

And what about the Valentine's Festival? His mask and black shirt had arrived in the mail that day, and they mocked him from his dresser where he'd set the package. Turning suddenly, he went downstairs and around the staircase to the den, practically ripping the door from the hinges he opened it so fiercely.

The dance floor sat in a neat stack in front of him, and he wondered how Logan planned to get it to the community center. He wasn't home from his job at the library yet, so Knox couldn't ask him.

Mortie whined at the back door, drawing Knox's attention away from the dance floor that was a physical manifestation of what he'd lost. He stepped over to the door and let the dog out, Rutabaga trotting over to go with Mortie.

He stood at the back door though it was freezing and hollered at them to hurry up. Mortie had suddenly gone deaf, because the dog took forever to sniff out the right spot and get things taken care of.

Logan's headlights cut through the darkness as Mortie trotted over, a doggy smile on his face as if he'd done something amazing. "Hey, bud," his twin said, bending down to scrub his dog. "Hey, Knox."

"How are we getting the dance floor to the community center?"

Logan groaned as he straightened, bracing one hand against his lower back. "In my truck. You'll be able to help?"

Knox hadn't been planning to help, but he wasn't sure he could go out to Quinn Valley on Valentine's Day. "Yes," he said, deciding on the spot that he could take the day off. Rhodes wouldn't have to know it was because of Betsy, who would also be busy at the community center that day.

"Great." Logan grinned at him, clapped him on the shoulder, and entered the house, his dog right behind him. "Should we order pizza for dinner?"

Knox closed the door. "Betsy broke up with me."

Logan spun from the fridge, lowering his phone from his ear. "What?"

"She said she doesn't see me in her future."

Logan wore concern on his face, and Knox sure did appreciate it. "I'm so sorry," he said. "You really liked her, and it seemed like you were getting along."

"I thought so," Knox said. "I mean, things weren't perfect. She made me mad once."

"Oh, boy," Logan said. "I can't even make you mad."

Knox ignored his brother and said, "Order some pizza. Maybe I'll be able to think clearer when I'm not starving."

But the pizza didn't help. Neither did explaining everything to Logan. And when he went back upstairs to bed, the package with his costume for the masquerade ball continued to mock him.

He lay in bed, wondering if he should simply skip the dance completely. Logan hadn't been counting on him to help with the floor, and he'd eaten plenty of Betsy's sugar cookies.

By morning, he hadn't decided. Sunday, he skipped church so he wouldn't make a scene in front of all the little old ladies he'd met a few weeks ago. Monday, he worked at Granite Falls, and Tuesday, he managed to spend the day in the stables and blacksmith shop without seeing a single Quinn. He didn't want to talk about Betsy, and while he wasn't sure if she'd have discussed their relationship with her older brother, he still stayed in a stall with a horse until Rhodes had left with Flynn.

Valentine's Day dawned with snow drifting down to the ground, and Knox was glad he didn't have to drive out to the ranch today. The weather canceled the work on the expansion of the library too, and the brothers enjoyed pancakes and eggs for breakfast.

"Are you going to go tonight?" Logan asked.

"That's the question of the hour, isn't it?" Knox sighed and speared another wedge of pancake. "I don't know."

"I think you should. Everyone will be masked. You haven't told her who you'll be. You could ask her to dance."

"She said she wouldn't have time to dance."

"And so that's it," Logan said, an undercurrent of disgust in his voice. "You're just going to let her go?"

"She's a grown woman. I already went and talked to her," he said. "That worked for you and Georgia, but it didn't work for me." Knox stabbed at his eggs, wishing they were his brother's fingers.

"She asked me not to tell you this, but...."

Knox looked up, morbid curiosity running through her. "What?"

Logan wouldn't look at him, and that only drove Knox closer to madness. As if the past week hadn't been a spectacular kind of torture, with nothing but frustration and no way to release it.

"She asked me to build her a house," Logan finally said. "I guess Rhodes gave her some land across the street from the cabins just inside the entrance."

Great, Knox thought. Now he'd have to drive past her house every time he went to work. "Are you going to do it?" he asked.

"I was going to talk to you first." Logan swallowed, his nerves clear. "I don't really want to build houses or work on library expansions. Georgia and I have been talking, and I want to buy a ranch of my own."

Shock moved through Knox like a sonic boom. "A ranch. Wow."

"I think you can afford this place on your own," he said. "Right?"

"Yeah, I'll be fine." His farrier salary was more than enough to pay the mortgage. That wasn't what he was worried about.

It was the utter and complete loneliness he'd have to endure once Logan moved out.

In that moment, he decided to go to the Valentine's masquerade ball, and he decided sending up a prayer that he could find another way to get Betsy back would manifest itself before then.

CHAPTER THIRTEEN

*B*etsy sat at the sewing machine, her shoulders aching from the hunched position she'd kept them in for so long. If she let her mind think about anything but the next step in making this dress, she'd deviate to Knox.

She pulled back on the tears as she thought about how he wouldn't even see this dress. She'd been designing and planning it for the Valentine's ball for weeks. Now she just needed to get all the pieces put together.

She felt like her whole life had shattered into a million tiny pieces since Knox had walked out the back door three days ago. She'd skipped church that morning, something she knew would have her whole family bunched together in whispered conversations. She expected a visit from her mother and Granny later.

But for now, she just sewed.

The homestead was quiet, only the whir of the furnace kicking on from time to time, and she enjoyed the peace that came from being alone. At the same time, her heart wailed that she'd always be alone now. That she'd had her perfect cowboy's hand in hers, and she'd cut him loose.

She exhaled and straightened, using the scissors to cut the thread as easily as she'd sliced Knox from her life.

"Stop it," she whispered to herself. She didn't want to live her whole life on eggshells, wondering if her husband resented her for simply getting to stay home and "do nothing." Even if her perspective on that was different—even if she saw homemakers as the hardest job with the least respect, even if she knew mothers held the home together—she couldn't make Knox see things her way.

He's never said that, she told herself as she looked at the panel she'd just sewn. The fabric was the color of eggplant skins, deep and dark and mysterious. She wanted it to feel romantic and light at the same time, so she'd bought cream lace to soften it up a little bit. Her mask covered the top half of her face and extended up into her hair to make an elegant pair of rabbit ears. They too, boasted a deep purple color with cream fur for the inside of the ears.

She'd been so excited about her costume, mostly to see Knox's reaction to her wearing it. But now, it only made her cry.

She set aside the panel she'd just finished and picked up the next pinned piece. The machine whirred. She kept her focus razor-sharp on the line she needed to stitch, and she didn't stop until she heard her sisters arrive home from church.

Only then did she line her pieces up along the six-foot table in the multi-purpose room she shared with Jessie. When she went into the kitchen, she found Georgia, Cami, and Jessie pulling boxed cereal out of the cupboards, along with spoons and gallons of milk.

"What are you doing?" she asked, joining them.

They froze, almost as if they hadn't been expecting her to be home. "Getting something to eat," Georgia said, exchanging a glance with Jessie.

"I have pizza," she said. "I just need to bake it off." She nudged Cami away from the fridge, gently taking the gallon of milk from her sister and setting it back in the door. She grabbed the two pizzas she'd made that morning and backed up. "See?"

"We weren't sure," Georgia said. "And you shouldn't have to cook for all of us all the time."

Fear stabbed right through Betsy. "I like cooking for all of us all the time." They couldn't take that away from her. If she couldn't feed people, what was her worth? Tears sprang to her eyes and she stepped over to the stove to set down the pizzas.

Her emotions would not be tamed, and she sucked in a breath that sounded dangerously like a sob.

"Oh, Betsy," Cami said, joining her. She put her arm around her, and Betsy's vision swam with tears as she set the oven temperature.

"It'll just be a half an hour," she said, her voice high and tight.

"Rhodes said he'd go for anything we want," Jessie said.

"I made pizza," Betsy said, turning to face her sisters. Tears streamed down her cheeks, and she hated that she was crying. But these were her sisters, and if she couldn't cry in front of them, who could she be real with?

"She made pizza," Cami said. "So someone call Rhodes and tell him to just get a couple of salads."

Betsy wiped her face, everything feeling too hot. Jessie stepped forward and wrapped her arms around her, and that undid any composure she may have had left. She cried into her taller sister's shoulder, glad when Georgia and Cami made it a group hug.

"It's okay," Jessie said. "Everything will be okay."

"How?" Betsy asked.

"You just need to talk to him," Georgia said.

"If you're this unhappy," Cami added. "You can change it. I think he'd be willing to get back together."

"Yeah," Jessie said. "*You* broke up with *him*."

The group embrace dissolved, and a flash of anger struck her like lightning. "I know what I did."

Her three sisters faced her, the few moments of silence stretching uncomfortable. Finally, Georgia said, "Then fix it." She glanced at Jessie and then Cami. "I'm going to go call Rhodes." She stepped away; the oven beeped, signaling it was to temperature; Betsy turned to put the pizzas in.

When she turned back around, she found Cami making punch and Jessie pulling down dishes. Activity filled the kitchen when Rhodes arrived with the salads, as well as Granny and Gramps. Betsy's parents arrived, and she accepted her father's hug, finding a bit of comfort there when it had eluded her previously.

With all the food on the counter, she'd normally step forward and go through all of it. But today, humiliation filled her and she just stood in the kitchen, a half-step behind Granny. Every eye landed on her, and she wanted to rage at her family.

She couldn't believe she'd messed up so badly. Regret lanced through her, and she just wanted to run away.

"Betsy made her barbecue chicken pizza," Granny said stepping forward. "It's got mushrooms, green peppers, and red onions." She gestured to the other pizza. "This one is a supreme. Looks like ham and sausage. Black olives, green peppers, and onions."

"Let's say grace," her father said, and Betsy folded her arms and closed her eyes unsurprised when tears trickled out of them. Her father's deep voice thanking the Lord for their blessings passed quickly, and then it was time to eat.

Betsy usually stood back and waited for everyone to serve themselves, and today was no exception. Gratitude for

Granny streamed through her, and she pressed her cheek to Granny's papery, powder-scented one, and whispered, "Thanks, Granny."

Then she slipped out of the kitchen, her appetite completely gone.

SHE FINISHED THE DRESS ON TUESDAY. SHOPPED FOR ALL the ingredients she needed for the refreshments on Wednesday. Posted one last reminder in all the online forums she could for the dance and other festivities going on in Quinn Valley for Valentine's Day.

And then Valentine's Day arrived, and there was nothing rosy or romantic about showing up at the pub at four o'clock in the morning and measuring flour and sugar to make cookies. Her eyes felt dry and scratchy, but she applied her focus to the baking, and she got all the sweets done and cooled before Bethany showed up.

"Made some caramels for you." She smiled at Betsy, who instantly felt bad she didn't have anything for the other woman. She took the box of candy and clutched it to her chest.

"Thank you, Bethany." She hugged her, and Bethany held her tight.

"I'm working all day and night, so good luck with the dance," she said, finally stepping back.

"Thanks," Betsy said. She loaded up everything she needed and headed back to the homestead to start on the cupcakes and cake pops. She worked upstairs and down, going back and forth to put in trays and then take them out. Put more in. Take more out.

Once everything was baked and cooling, she whipped together the cream cheese frosting and a batch of buttercream. With all the parts ready and waiting—except for the candy melts she was using to coat the cake pops—she showered, giving the cakes all the time they needed to cool properly.

As she came back into the kitchen fully made up and with her hair completely straight, all she needed to do was frost, crumble, dip, and decorate.

Half of the three hundred cupcakes got pink frosting and half got purple. She swirled from a piping bag, and she'd bought chocolates in the shape of hearts for the decoration. She was already killing herself in a lot of ways, and she didn't need to temper chocolate and pipe hearts and arrows.

She filled trays with thirty-six cupcakes and took them into the garage to make sure everything would be set for traveling later that day.

Crumbling up cake for the cake pops came next, and she enjoyed getting her hands messy as she mixed in the frosting to make the balls stick together. She scooped them out with a premeasured scoop and speared them all on sticks. She had brightly colored decorating sugar in pink and red, as well as some big sprinkles in a variety of bright, spring colors.

She stirred and melted, melted and stirred. Then she dipped, and dipped, and dipped, rolling some pops in the sugar and sprinkling others.

By four o'clock, she never wanted to see another cupcake or cake pop in her life. But she had three hundred cake pops lined up in blocks of Styrofoam, and when Jessie came in the kitchen, she stopped and whistled.

"Betsy," she said, taking in the scene on the counter. "These are beautiful."

"Thank you," she said. "I have to leave in an hour." She moved into the living room and collapsed onto the couch. "I just have to change, so I'm going to lay here for a few minutes."

"You said you'd do my makeup," Jessie said.

"You don't need it," Betsy said. "It's a *masquerade* ball."

"I'm going to shower," Jessie said as if Betsy hadn't even spoken. With silence back in the homestead and Betsy finally done with her baking, she let her mind wander.

Of course, it went straight to Knox, and she toyed with the idea of texting him. Just to ask if he'd be at the dance that night. Maybe mention that she'd love to see him, talk to him, find a way back to him.

She couldn't bring herself to do it, though, because it felt unfair of her. She couldn't just expect him to come running whenever she texted. Then walk away when she got scared or paranoid or unsure of herself and her life choices.

"You are who you are," she whispered to herself. And she couldn't skip the dance, so she got up, got dressed, and did Jessie's makeup before loading up all of her confections and following Georgia as she drove with Jessie and Cami to the dance.

She kept her fingers tight around the wheel, and her eyes glued to the worsening roads as the snow continued to fall. This weather would keep people home rather than bringing them out to the dance, and she worried that she'd made way too many refreshments. With every passing moment, her mind churned through a constant prayer.

Let there be a lot of people there. Help me arrive safely. Please bless Knox to come. Help others to enjoy my treats.

Let there be a lot of people there....

CHAPTER FOURTEEN

Knox normally didn't dress in all black clothing, and he felt very much like he could be anyone in these clothes. He supposed that was the object of a masquerade ball—people could be anyone—but he didn't particularly like it.

He arrived early with Logan to get the dance floor set up, using his muscles for the first time that day, and then ducked down the hall to the bathroom to change. When he went back into the gym, Betsy had arrived. She and her sisters, plus Logan, stood at the refreshment table, setting out trays and plates and tiered decorations.

He ducked behind one of the draperies Rhonda had set up surrounding the newly laid floor and peered through a crack. It was much too early to be at the dance as a regular attendee, and he wasn't ready to see Betsy yet.

She wore a beautiful dress that swelled and flowed in all the right ways. The sleeves billowed with each movement, and he wondered what the smooth fabric would feel like beneath his fingers.

She'd sewn lace over the bodice, and Knox's heart thundered in his chest. He wanted to spend Valentine's Day with her. He hated that she'd made all those gorgeous desserts alone. That he hadn't at least texted her. Could he still do it? Would she even have time to look at her phone?

As he watched from behind the curtain, he realized how empty his life had been this past week compared to when he'd been with Betsy. She was his first thought, and the only person he wanted to share his life with. The good things, the bad things, all the things.

Perhaps he should just walk over to her and tell her he loved her.

He sucked in a breath and ducked out of the gym, pulling off his Phantom mask as he went. He'd never been in love before, but he had no other words for the feelings streaming through him.

He found a small room down the hall that the dance committee had met in before, and he stepped inside. He could hide out here until more people arrived at the dance.

The witching hour arrived, and the noise level down the hall increased. The music started, and the dance was underway. Still Knox hid in the dark room, the only light splashing in from the hall.

His phone buzzed, and he hoped it would be Betsy but the better bet would be Logan. Sure enough, his brother's name sat on the screen, and he'd asked where Knox had disappeared to.

They'd driven over in Logan's red pickup truck, so Knox couldn't leave even if he wanted to. Half of him wanted to. The other half was still trying to decide if he should go back in there and...do something.

He inhaled, Logan's advice to him steaming through his mind. At this point, he didn't have anything else to lose. He strapped his mask into place and entered the hall, his cape fluttering behind him as he marched toward the dance.

"Cool," someone said as he joined the line from the wrong direction. They wore jeans and a T-shirt, a gold mask full of sparkle and glitter concealing who they were. He waited as the line edged forward, and then he was inside the darkened gym. Tea lights rimmed the top of all the draperies, and a decorative street lamp stood over by the refreshment table now.

He didn't see Betsy over there, but surely she wouldn't have migrated too far from making sure there were enough cake pops or sugar cookies on the platters and tiers. Sure enough, she sat in a chair to the left of the table, almost behind the last drape on that side.

She'd added a mask to her outfit, and it went up and over her head to make a pair of ears that simply took his breath away.

Still, he didn't go over to her. Someone said something to him, and he turned toward Flynn, a cowboy from the ranch. He wore a Batman mask with a Batman T-shirt and black jeans. Knox couldn't help chuckling, even if a pinch of jealousy hit him over the fact that Flynn got to see Betsy at poker night.

They chatted for a few minutes, and then Knox nodded toward the four masked women hovering a few feet away. "I think they're here for you, Batman," he said. Flynn glanced at them, and then back to Knox, a look of unrest in his eyes. Or maybe it was too dark to tell, because when Flynn turned back to his female admirers, he spoke in a bright, jovial voice.

Knox turned back to the refreshment table, his heart seeming to scream at him to go find Betsy and tell her everything.

She was gone.

Knox scanned the wall behind the refreshment table and

saw all the remaining treats. There weren't as many people as he'd expected to see, and everyone wore a mask. But he knew what Betsy was wearing, and she wasn't on the dancefloor either.

Surely she hadn't left the building completely.

His heart tapped and pittered, skipping over some beats and then racing forward with too many. He'd waited too long, and now she was gone.

The song ended, and the people dancing clapped. "Welcome to our masquerade ball," a woman said, and Knox spun, trying to find where Betsy was speaking into the microphone. He couldn't see her. Where was she?

"The costume contest will go until eight-thirty," she continued. "So be sure to cast your votes in the box by the refreshment table." Another song started to play, and Knox expected to see Betsy emerge from behind a curtain. Something.

He couldn't find her.

"There you are," Logan said, appearing at his side, Georgia's hand in his. She immediately started texting, and a few seconds later, the song stopped abruptly.

"I'm sorry," Betsy said. "But I have another announcement, ladies and gentlemen." A spotlight burst to life, shining on the stage in front of Knox. The curtains there continued the semi-circle that had been started on the floor, and they parted. Betsy stepped out, letting the spotlight illuminate her and her shiny, beautiful dress.

Knox only breathed because it was an involuntary response. He took a step forward without expressly telling himself to do so.

"I know this is a masquerade ball, and the point is to not know who you're dancing with. But I've made a terrible mistake, and I'm searching for someone specific so I can fix things." She drew in a deep breath, her eyes still focused straight ahead.

"So, Knox Locke, if you're in the room, could you please come forward?"

People started twittering and turning to look for him. Knox felt frozen to the floor, wanting to move forward but unsure how.

"Go on," Logan hissed, practically pushing him from behind.

"He's right here," Georgia called, and everyone turned to stare at him. Everything Knox disliked happened at once. He'd lived his life in the shadows, and as the spotlight trained on him, he was definitely uncomfortable.

He did manage to get his legs moving toward the stage, and Betsy pointed to the side, where he knew there were steps leading up to the stage. He detoured that way, ducking behind the curtain as another song started to play.

Thankfully. At least it seemed like they'd be having their talk in private. No microphone. No spotlight. No stage.

He made it to the steps and glanced up to see her standing at the top. She took his breath away, and time froze for a moment. He felt as if he was looking up at a princess, and he knew he didn't want to live another day without her in his life.

She came down the steps, a heart-shaped sugar cookie with pink frosting in her hand. She extended it toward him with the words, "I have made a terrible mistake."

He took the cookie and bit into it. It was melty and flaky and sweet. "I don't know," he said. "This tastes great."

Betsy smiled, but it wobbled around the edges. Her eyes burned brightly behind her mask, and she took another step toward him. "You asked me what I wanted for my life."

"I'm regretting asking that," he said, hoping this conversation was going to end better than the previous one on this same topic.

"I'm not," she said. "It really got me thinking. And doubting. But not everyone can be a doctor or a lawyer or own a ranch or a spa or a pub." She pressed her fingertips together. "And I just want to be a homemaker. I like sewing and cooking and gardening. I like decorating, and I think I'd be a good mom. I'm really good at organizing things, and I'd love to be in our home, waiting for you to finish shoeing whatever horse has been naughty so you can come home and relax."

Tears came over the front of her mask, and she reached up to remove it.

"I love you, Knox, and I just got scared that I might not be good enough for you, because what I want to do with my life doesn't earn anything, at least in terms of dollars and cents." She bit her bottom lip and swiped at her eyes. "I want that to be good enough for you, but I understand if it's not."

Knox didn't hesitate when he said, "It's always been good enough, Betsy. More than good enough." He set his cookie on the steps and swept his arms around her. "And I'm sorry I ever gave you the impression that it wasn't."

She reached up and touched his mask, and he took it off. "I love you too." He leaned down and kissed her, his pulse finally settling and his heart rejoicing that God had provided a path to understanding between the two of them.

He pulled away but continued to hold her close to his heart. "So you're going to build a house of your own on the ranch?"

"That was one idea," she said. "But Logan turned me down."

"He's buying a ranch," he said. "I'm not sure when, but by the time we're ready to get married, I bet he'll be gone. Maybe the house I have in town is acceptable to you?"

"I want to see it in the spring," she said, pulling back and gazing up at him, a playful edge in those beautiful eyes now.

"That's fine," he said.

She giggled and shook her head. "I'm sure it will be great, Knox. I just want to be where you are." She sobered, tipped up and kissed him, and Knox felt the same way.

He just wanted to be where she was.

CHAPTER FIFTEEN

Betsy laughed as Mortie and Roo romped around the yard, the sun shining merrily overhead. She'd been doing some landscaping at the Locke brother's house over the past couple of weeks, and she wanted to get these shrubs planted before Knox got home.

She wasn't sure why he disliked his brother's dogs so much. They were sweet, and after they tired themselves out, they'd find a nice patch of shade and keep her company while she worked.

She'd already started working on Knox to get a dog of their own once they were married—but that would require a proposal first. Logan and Georgia had just gotten engaged about two weeks ago, and Betsy told herself she simply needed to wait.

Georgia deserved to have her moment in the spotlight, and their mother had pulled out all the stops and made a wedding binder.

So Betsy had employed her patience. But she sure did want her own wedding binder, one with a picture of her and

Knox in the front, the way Georgia had one of her and Logan in it.

But for now, she was putting in a row of evergreen shrubs along the back fence at Knox's house. Logan and Georgia had also found a ranch, and once they were married, they'd be living out there, leaving the white, two-story house to Knox.

And hopefully Betsy with him, very soon.

She loved the smell of earth, the rich color of it, the way she could move it and transform it into something she wanted to add beauty to a place. So she leveled, and dug, and planted, and by the time Knox's truck purred into the driveway, she was sufficiently satisfied with her afternoon of work.

"Look at that," he said, coming to stand beside her on the lawn. Mortie and Roo jogged over to meet him, and he patted them, so maybe there was some hope for Betsy to get a dog after she and Knox were married.

"They're blue firs," she said. "They look great, and they smell great."

"I like them," Knox said. He leaned over and pressed a kiss to her temple. "I'm going to go shower, because wow, it's hot today, and then we can go to dinner if you want."

"I made dinner," she said.

"At my house?"

"You have a Crock pot," she said. "You probably just didn't know it." She bumped him with her hip and grinned up at him.

"Fourth of July picnic with your family tomorrow?" he asked.

"Yep," she said.

"All right." He walked to the back door, calling, "You made pulled pork sandwiches? I love you, Betsy!" when he reached the door.

And while it wasn't the most romantic time he'd told her he loved her, Betsy still felt the words curl her toes. Because she knew Knox loved her—and she loved him too. She cleaned up in the backyard before following Knox inside the house. She washed up in the kitchen and wandered over to the room behind the stairs.

This house was a cute home, but the space was interesting. The kitchen and dining room took up the back of the house, with a walk through opening into the living room. The steps sat right through that wide arched doorway, and they led up to three bedrooms and two bathrooms.

The front door led right into the living room, and on the other side of the steps was a small half-bath. It certainly wasn't as big as the homestead, but the house sat on half an acre, and Betsy knew she could be happy here.

Knox came downstairs, smelling and looking fresh, and she went into the kitchen to get dinner served.

"You're the best," he said as he loaded cole slaw on top of his barbecue pork.

"Don't be too excited," she said. "I had to make all of this because it's what we're eating at the family barbecue tomorrow too."

"Still." He took a big bite of his sandwich, and Betsy nudged a folder closer to him.

"I was thinking of adding in a patio," she said, leaving her cole slaw as a side dish. "The backyard is spectacular, and it would be nice to be able to eat out there sometimes. Picnic. Have a fire pit. Dutch oven cooking."

He looked at her designs, appreciation shining in his eyes. "This looks great, Bets. You can totally do this."

"Okay." She swept the papers back into the folder. "I'll keep it in mind for once we're married."

Knox's gaze flew to hers, and she gave him a look she hoped said, *Well? When's that going to happen?*

"Logan and Georgia set a date," she said. "My mother asked me when she'd have wedding number two."

"I thought you wanted a spring wedding."

"I do," she said. "Idaho is lovely in the spring. Georgia's getting married at Christmastime, as if there aren't enough Quinn Family parties at that time of year. I think my mom would be able to help with another wedding by April or May."

"Then let's do April or May," he said.

"That's not how it works, Knox," she said, shaking her head. They'd had this conversation before.

"Tell me how it works," he said, right on cue.

She giggled, but a part of her cried in frustration. "You have to ask me first."

He simply smiled and took another bite of his sandwich.

THE FOLLOWING DAY, BETSY GOT UP EARLY AND GOT TO work in the kitchen. Her experience at the pub at four a.m. had been good for something. But it was so much easier to get up early in the summer, because the sun was waking too.

She set about making the hamburger buns from scratch, anticipating a huge crowd as all the Quinns from all five of Granny and Gramps's children came to the Fourth of July picnic. Georgia joined her to get the Crock pots plugged in and the pork heating slowly.

Betsy tried not to be jealous about the glinting diamond on her finger, but it was impossible. She allowed herself a few minutes of envy, and then Bethany and Ryder arrived. After that, it seemed like a constant stream of arrivals, and hugs, and exclamations over new boyfriends and fiancés.

Granny finally called for everyone to go outside, and the picnic table got laden with dozens of bowls, bottles, and bags. Chips and ketchup and salads. Baked beans. Pulled pork. Cole slaw. Every new bowl made Betsy's heart sing a little louder.

Gramps stood at the head of the long row of picnic tables, the hubbub and chatter seemingly impossible to quiet. But Rhodes whistled, and that got everyone to quiet down and look in the right direction.

"We love having you all out here at the ranch," Gramps said. "What a great tradition this is." His voice cracked, and Betsy's heart swelled with love for her grandparents. For the extended family. For this heritage her ancestors had built in Quinn Valley.

"I don't normally do a big speech, and I'm not going to this year," he continued. "But there's someone who has something he wants to say." Gramps nodded to someone down the row, and then he sat down.

To Betsy's great astonishment, Knox rose from the bench about halfway down the first picnic table. Her heart immediately tried to fling itself free of her ribcage, and when his eyes met hers, the whole world fell away.

"Can I get you to come up here, Betsy?" Knox didn't talk in a loud voice, but every Quinn eye was riveted to him. It felt like a very long walk to the head of the table, where Betsy sometimes stood to explain food. But she didn't like the spotlight as much as she used to, and heat filled her cheeks.

"I promise this will be fast," he said. "I know we're all hungry." He turned to her, a wide smile on his face. "I'm in love with you, and I want to spend the rest of my life with you. It's not a secret, and it never will be."

He dropped to both knees right there on the grass and grabbed a box perched on the end of the picnic table. "Will you marry me?"

The whole table erupted, and Quinns were not known for being quiet. The cheers and applause felt like they filled the whole sky, Betsy's whole soul.

She laughed at the same time she cried, and she managed to say "Yes," even amidst all the chaos.

　　　　　　　　　　LIZ ISAACSON

Knox slid the ring on her shaking fingers and took her face in his hands. He looked right into her eyes and said, "I love you, Betsy Quinn," just before kissing her.

Betsy rejoiced as she kissed him back, and when he broke the kiss and leaned his forehead against hers, she said, "I love you too."

Read on for a sneak peek of **<u>Landscaping Love</u>, now available in paperback!**

And keep reading to get the coveted Quinn family recipe for ham, egg and cheese breakfast sliders! Serve it at your next family gathering...or for brunch. Whatever. :)

HAM, EGG, & CHEESE BREAKFAST SLIDERS

Ham, Egg, & Cheese Breakfast Sliders

1 pkg (12 count) Hawaiian Rolls

8 - 10 eggs (depending on egg size & how "eggy" you want your sliders)

6 large slices provolone cheese

Sliced ham

¼ Cup butter, melted

1 Tbsp yellow mustard

1 Tbsp brown sugar

1. Scramble up your eggs however you like to do them.
2. While the eggs scramble, cut the entire package of rolls in half (so you have a sheet of the tops & the bottoms).
3. Place the bottom sheet of rolls in a pan and top with a thin layer of provolone cheese.

4. Once the eggs are done, cover the cheese layer with the eggs. Lay ham slices over the eggs. If your provolone is nice & thin, then you can add two more slices over the eggs and then again over the ham.

5. Place the top sheet of rolls over the ham.

6. In a small bowl, combine melted butter, mustard & brown sugar. Stir until well combined and the sugar is mostly dissolved. Then coat the tops of the rolls with the mixture.

7. Bake at 350 for 15 minutes (until cheese gets nice & melty).

8. Remove from oven and let cool a few minutes. Then cut, serve, and enjoy!

*C*apri Haywood sucked in a breath, her eyes taking in the dilapidated condition of the house.

"See how the wood's rotted here?"

She saw it, and she nodded at the man who'd met her to let her in the house. It was only a rental, but it was also the only place Capri had to stay that night. Her emotions choked her, making breathing difficult.

"Ma'am, do you have somewhere else you can stay?" he asked.

She shook her head, tight little bursts of movement that felt like they'd crack her neck. Splinter her spine.

"I can't believe Parker thought he could rent this place," Gerald said, shaking his head. "There's not even carpet on the floor."

Capri let her eyes sweep over the concrete before she turned away. Quinn Valley was turning out to be as bad as Crescent Lake.

No, she told herself as she went down the front steps. Nothing would be as bad as staying in Crescent Lake.

"Is there a hotel?" she managed to ask, her voice so unlike her own.

"Sure thing." Gerald looked at the truck and trailer Capri had pulled all the way from Texas. Exhaustion ran through her at the thought of trying to park the outfit somewhere in town. Maybe she could leave it here. Grab her suitcase from the back and have Gerald take her to the hotel.

He was an older gentleman, probably in his late fifties, and he lived just down the road from the house. "The Quinn Hotel and Spa," he said. "Best in town, and it's close to everything."

"Probably not the ranch," she said, looking at Gerald out of the corner of her eye. "Right?'

"Oh, no, not the ranch," he said, shaking his head. "That's north of here. Twenty minutes or so. Can't miss it."

Capri was sure of that, as the owner had said the same thing. She'd been planning to get settled in her house and take a quick trip out to the ranch, just to see it. Get a feel for the land and this new place she was about to call home.

But now there would be no settling in that house. What was she going to do with all her stuff? Her furniture, her bed, her boxes of Christmas décor?

The very idea that she'd brought the blue and gold balls was ludicrous. But Capri had lost a lot in Crescent Lake, and she'd held onto the stupidest of things simply because she could.

"Do you need a ride?" Gerald asked?

"No," Capri said, deciding on the spot. "Maybe you could help me unhitch the trailer? Then I can just leave it here while I figure out what to do."

"Sure thing," he said again, and he got to work. He had the trailer off and steady in about a third of the time Capri would've been able to do it, and gratitude swept through her. He would be in her gratitude journal that night.

She only wrote one thing for each day, but today would be the helpfulness of Gerald Neis. It had taken her four days to drive to Quinn Valley, Idaho from southern Texas, and each day she'd experienced a little miracle.

Gerald was hers today.

"Thanks so much," she said, forcing a smile to her lips. Such an action used to be easy, something she did without thinking. But now, after the indictment, the failed business, the lost job, the break-up....

Capri didn't have much left to smile about. And yet, God had provided a way for her to have at least one sentence of gratitude each day.

She made it back to the downtown area of Quinn Valley, enjoying the quaint atmosphere of the street. It looked like it had been plucked from the beginning of a Hallmark movie, and a sense of peace stole through Capri.

The hotel and spa sat on her left, but she went past them so she could check out the rest of the street, see what the town had to offer as far as shopping and dining. There was a pub, which looked promising, and a row of shops where she could surely kill a few hours on a Saturday afternoon.

If she wasn't too busy catching up on sleep or managing her brand-new business. "Yeah, you're not going to be shopping on the weekends," she muttered to herself. She'd probably be working. Getting new clients. Researching the fauna that thrived in this new place.

Her stomach growled, reminding Capri that she hadn't eaten since breakfast, and that had been on the southern border of Utah, eight hours ago. Up ahead, she saw a huge hamburger, with plenty of bacon hanging out the side.

Yep, that would be her first dining experience here in Quinn Valley. The Bacon Boys looked busy, but at least her truck didn't stand out among the dozen other pickups in the parking lot.

It was several years old, and the best she could afford. In fact, she hoped the prices for beef and bacon in this town wouldn't break her budget, as she was down to her last two hundred dollars.

"Be right back, Mols," she said to her black and white Boston terrier. "I'll get you something." But she probably wouldn't. She'd just feed the dog a couple of bites of her burger and most of the French fries.

It's okay, she told herself as she got out of the truck and headed inside. *You have a job. Starts tomorrow.*

And she did. She was meeting the ranch's owner at nine o'clock, and everything would be fine.

Her momma's words streamed through her head. *You're a real good girl, Capri. Everything will be fine.*

She'd clung to her momma's promises in the past, and she'd do the same thing this time too.

Inside the burger joint, the atmosphere was vibrant and smelled like everything Capri imagined heaven would. Cheese and beef and bacon.

And boys.

So many men filled the place that Capri wondered if she'd missed a sign somewhere. *Men only*, or *No cowboy hat, no service*.

Capri didn't fit either of those requirements, and she felt the full weight of every eye on her as she joined the line.

This place was obviously popular for four o'clock in the afternoon, and she anticipated having to wait several minutes to put in her order.

It's fine, she told herself, the eyes finally going back to their own business. Her head pounded, and her stomach pinched, but she studied the menu as if she'd never eaten a hamburger before.

She'd eat, and everything would be better.

Then she'd go to the hotel and figure out if she could even

afford to stay for a night. Quinn Valley Ranch had offered her a cabin as part of her pay, but she'd declined it. Maybe she'd need to ask the owner about that too.

Her head swam with all she needed to do and figure out. Capri wanted to bolt right then, but she held steady in the line. Her daddy had taught her that. Wait. Watch. Listen. Learn.

She'd be putting all of those things to use as she started her own landscaping company a thousand miles from the only home she'd ever known.

The door behind her chimed, indicating someone new had walked in. She turned to find a tall cowboy coming in alone. He exuded an air of importance, keeping her attention on him. A smile flashed across his face, making his strong jaw a little softer and lighting his eyes from within.

Oh, that wasn't fair.

Capri was well-versed in handsome cowboys, but this guy was in a league all his own.

She couldn't help how her eyes dropped to his left hand to check for a wedding band. He wasn't wearing one.

So he's fair game, she thought, immediately recoiling from it. She was not looking for a new boyfriend. She had barely escaped Texas with her most vital organ still intact.

She half-turned, expecting this handsome man to come stand right behind her. Maybe she could ask him what was good here, explain she was new in town, all of that.

But he didn't. Instead, he went right past her, almost to the front of the line.

"Uh, excuse me?" she said before she could even think.

In the Hallmark movie, the record would've scratched. The chatter in the place halted, and everyone turned toward her.

"The line's back here," she said, her eyes blazing at that cowboy. Just because he was good-looking didn't mean he could do whatever he wanted. Maybe it was the extreme hunger talking. Or the pounding headache. Or the fact that the house she'd rented—and put a thousand dollars down on —was filled with termites and completely unlivable.

Or, or, or. Capri could honestly come up with a dozen other reasons she wouldn't be putting up with a cowboy cutting in line.

"I'm sorry," he said, looking at the men he'd joined. "I was just taking a phone call. My guys here saved my spot." He had the charming ability to look confused and ashamed at the same time, that confidence still oozing off of him in waves.

Capri cocked her hip and then stepped around the few people between them. "Fine. My guys were just holding my spot too." She looked to his equally tall, hatted, and obviously baffled friends. "Right guys?"

"Right," one mumbled before turning back to the cashier and putting in his order. Capri stayed right with them, ordering when they all did. She cocked her eyebrow at the handsome man who'd pushed the wrong button with the wrong woman today—and watched in horror as he paid for everyone.

Including her.

So he really was there with those guys, and he was most likely their boss. "You don't—"

"You're one of the guys," he said easily. "Don't worry about it." Then he joined his crew at the soda fountain, never once looking back at her.

Capri huddled near the door, snatching her bag as soon as the teenager brought it to her and hurrying back to the safety of her truck and her dog. The burger tasted like manna from heaven, and with one problem solved, she went to take care of another, praying the hotel would allow pups for just one night.

❄

THE FOLLOWING MORNING, SHE LEFT THE HOTEL MUCH
earlier than she needed to. Her nerves fired on all cylinders,
and no amount of positive self-talk and family mantras could
soothe her. Aurora usually kept her up-to-date on such things,
and while Capri had spoken with her sister at length once
she'd made it to the hotel last night, all the good vibes were
now gone.

The ranch was exactly twenty minutes north of town, and
she eased her truck under the sign boasting that she'd arrived
at Quinn Valley Ranch.

"Twenty minutes early," she muttered, moving slowly past
the row of cabins on her left, paying close attention to the
way she felt here. It wasn't Texas, that was for sure, but this
land felt...tranquil. And that was exactly what Capri needed
in her life right now.

A purpose. A place.

Next to her on the seat, Molly whined, her paws up on
the window on the passenger side. Capri pushed the button
to roll down the window, smiling at Molly's exuberance as she
stuck her head outside.

She rumbled down the road and pulled up to the homestead, a thin line of dust rising into the air behind her. She'd
heard Idaho was cold, but this late in May, it seemed to be
warm enough for her.

"Let's go," she said to Molly, and they got out of the truck
together. No one had come to greet her, and she reminded
herself that she was early. Before she could decide if she
should go knock on the front door or just sit tight for a few
minutes, another truck came down the road.

He parked beside her, and Capri's eyes met his through
the windshield.

"Oh, no," she moaned under her breath as the tall, delicious, drink-of-water cowboy who'd paid for her dinner yesterday got out of his truck.

Her eyes flew to the porch as the screech of the screen door sounded. Maybe he was just here for something else, perhaps a visit.

"I got it, Dad," he said, his deep voice sending vibrations through Capri's whole body. He definitely wasn't just visiting, and he was definitely her new boss.

Can Rhodes and Capri landscape their love? Or will they go their separate ways once the yard is finished? **Find out in __LANDSCAPING LOVE__ - available in paperback!**

Contracted Cowboy (Book 1): A fake ad brings a cowboy to Georgia's door just in time for all the Quinn family holiday parties, so she hires Logan to be her boyfriend. Nothing can go wrong with this plan...except she might lose her heart to her newly contracted cowboy.

Secret Sweetheart (Book 2): She's a domestic goddess. He works on her father's ranch. They could have forever...if they could take their relationship out of the shadows. **Can she overcome her anxiety and fear and build a life with Knox? Or will their relationship be doomed to die in the shadows at Quinn Valley Ranch?**

Landscaping Love (Book 3): He hired her to landscape the yard, but she's going to make him re-evaluate who he lets into his heart. **Can Rhodes and Capri landscape their love? Or will they go their separate ways once the yard is finished?**

Birthday Boyfriend (Book 4): This Quinn cowgirl doesn't need a lot for her birthday...just the cowboy she's been crushing on for months. Will Flynn ever see Jessie standing right in front of him?

Fall Fireside (Book 5): Cami Quinn has had enough of being the shiny new date for the cowboys in Quinn Valley. She's on her fifth or sixth broken heart, and she needs the soothing, healing messages she's found at the fall fireside series in the past. Will Cami and Clay find a way to mend what's broken inside themselves in order to find a happily-ever-after?

ABOUT LIZ

Liz Isaacson writes inspirational romance, usually set in Texas, or Wyoming, or anywhere else horses and cowboys exist. She lives in Utah, where she writes full-time, takes her two dogs to the park everyday, and eats a lot of veggies while writing. Find her on her website at feelgoodfictionbooks.com